BLINDED

BLINDED

TRAVIS THRASHER

MOODY PUBLISHERS
CHICAGO

ISBN: 0-8024-8672-X
ISBN-13: 978-0-8024-8672-1

Cover Design: LeVan Fisher Design
Cover Image: Steven Puetzer/Masterfile
Interior Design: LeftCoast Design
Editors: LB Norton and Ali Diaz

Library of Congress Cataloging-in-Publication Data

Thrasher, Travis, 1971-
    Blinded / by Travis Thrasher.
        p. cm.
    ISBN-13: 978-0-8024-8672-1
    ISBN-10: 0-8024-8672-X
    1. Husbands—Fiction. 2. Temptation—Fiction. 3. Manhattan
(New York, N.Y.)—Fiction.   I. Title.

PS3570.H6925B55 2006
813'.6—dc22

                                        2006014340

We hope you enjoy this book from Moody Publishers. Our goal is to
provide high-quality, thought-provoking books and products that
connect truth to your real needs and challenges. For more information on other books and products written and produced from a bib-
lical perspective, go to www.moodypublishers.com or write to:

Moody Publishers
820 N. LaSalle Boulevard
Chicago, IL 60610

1 3 5 7 9 10 8 6 4 2

For Ben, Brandon, Jeremy, Mark, and Scott.

Five men who will always have my respect.

In New York freedom looks like too many choices
In New York I found a friend to drown out the other voices

—"New York" by U2

4:47 P.M.

"MIND IF I JOIN YOU?"

These are not the words you expect to hear. Not now, on a Friday midafternoon in Manhattan. Not after the two days you've had. Not after the cancelled dinner and the cancelled merger. And positively, definitely, not from the beautiful woman in the black skirt and heels standing before you.

For a moment you're lost for words. You're never lost for words. But for half a second, you can't say anything.

Only half an hour ago you watched her settle into her seat and order a glass of wine and cross her legs and gaze out at the sidewalk close to Rockefeller Center. Sipping a red and people-watching, just as you were doing. Your glance shifted, first to the table in front of you, then to the half-glass of Pinot Grigio, then the empty chair facing you, then the glisten of your wedding ring in the sun. But your eyes found their way back to the blonde sitting in front of you, her profile in full view, her eyes glancing over and easily spotting your gaze.

You were the first to look away.

This sort of fun, innocent glancing went on for half an hour as the motion of the city blurred behind. People getting off work, tourists roaming, couples strolling. You are here because you've ordered wine from this place before. It's a hobby you've only picked up the last couple of years; harmless, yet you keep it from some of the couples you know. Some of your church friends who still make a big deal out of drinking. But in a city far away from the suburbs of Chicago, nobody is going to see you. Nobody is going to care if you're on your second glass. Or if you're staring at one of the hottest women you've ever seen.

It doesn't hurt to look.

But for some reason she's now standing in front of you, looking down at you, smiling, waiting for an answer.

"Go ahead."

That's all you say.

She sits down across from you, a glass in her hand. For a moment she continues watching the sidewalk.

You have no idea how your life is about to change.

Full lips that curl into a smile captivate you. You wait for her to say something.

"Enjoying your glass?"

"Very much," you reply.

"What do you have?"

"A Pinot Grigio."

Her voice is soft but confident, more mature than her twenty-something appearance suggests.

"Much of a wine connoisseur?"

You shake your head and ask, "Are you?"

"I come here to observe people. It's always fascinating who you might run into."

Her soft, flawless skin almost glows.

"Where are you from?" she asks after a moment of silence.

"Do I look like a tourist?"

"You don't look like a New Yorker."

"Chicago," you say. It's easier than saying Deerfield, Illinois.

"You don't have an accent."

"Neither do you."

"I haven't stuck around anywhere long enough to pick up an accent."

Her greenish-blue eyes, model's eyes, would seem manufactured if they were in a magazine. Blonde hair that might be real or colored falls several inches below her shoulders. The look she gives is confident, curious, and relaxed.

You think it's a dangerous look. Women might be the ones who claim to have intuitions, but you have some yourself.

"Where are you from?"

"Florida. And California."

"Which one first?"

She shines another smile. "Does it matter?"

"No."

"Florida," she answers.

A waiter comes up, and she preempts his question by ordering another glass of something called The Prisoner.

"That's the name of a wine?"

She nods. You tell the waiter you'll try a glass.

It's the end of a long week and you didn't ask for her to be sitting there and there's nothing wrong with sharing a glass of wine with a stranger in the middle of hundreds of other strangers. A single snapshot might look scandalous but you have an explanation and you don't need an explanation anyway.

You're too fried to even think about anything except wondering who this woman is and what she really wants.

"Heading back soon?" she asks.

She has a strong voice. Nothing about her is weak. Her gaze doesn't waver as you keep your eyes on hers and avoid looking at anything else. Or any other part of her.

"Tomorrow."

"So with all the sights to see in New York, and all the things to do, what brings you here?"

"I order wines from this place. Thought I'd check it out in person."

"First time to New York?"

"First time sitting here," you tell her.

You came to New York first with Lisa.

Lisa is your wife, just in case you need someone to remind you.

The blonde takes a sip from her wine and you look at her lips for a second longer than you probably should.

I'm tired, you think. *Tired and fed up and not wanting to think.*

Perhaps this is rationalizing.

"And you're all alone?"

Now you're the one to smile.

"Am I missing something here?" you ask.

"Uncomfortable with questions?"

"I've seen stuff like this on television shows. People getting pranked."

"I just figured you might like some company. And I thought you probably wouldn't take the initiative to join me."

"And you're all alone?" you repeat her question.

"At the moment, no. Just making light conversation to pass the time."

You wonder if this is a New York thing.

"I'm Michael," you tell her, finally being friendly.

"And what does Michael do for a living?"

You smile. "Michael works in technology."

"You sell it?"

"Does it matter?" you ask, teasing her.

"Come on. You already told me your name."

"I could've made up it up. There are thousands of Michaels."

"There are thousands of salesmen."

"I don't sell anything. I'm a VP of finance. It's a small company."

Hoping to be bought out by a conglomerate. Hoping to capitalize on growth. Hoping to seal a deal that would set me for life.

Hope has many meanings. You don't want to think about hope anymore.

"You don't look like the accountant type."

"Trust me, I'm not."

She looks at you and doesn't look away. The sidewalks are getting busier but you've stopped watching people.

"So what are *you* selling?" you ask.

Her gaze doesn't waver. "Please."

"What?"

"A lot of women might take that as an insult."

"A lot of guys might be too stupid to ask."

She sips her glass again and for the moment continues to watch the crowd. As if she's done, at least for the moment, with the conversation. You don't know if she's out on business, but she might be. Wearing a suit with the skirt cut above her knees and a white blouse that looks expensive. Black pointy heels. A little purse that can only carry sunglasses and a couple of credit cards.

This is the way your luck goes. A beautiful outgoing

woman with that look in her eye comes and sits down at a table with you to share a glass of wine and some light banter. There is nothing more that can happen because you are a married man with two children. And Lisa might wonder what in the world you're doing with this woman in the first place, talking and smiling and sharing a glass of wine.

It's harmless and you didn't do anything to prompt it and nothing else will come of it because nothing *can* come of it. And that's your luck. Because as beautiful as this woman is, she is not yours and can never be yours and all she will be is a seductive smile to look at.

"Tell me, Michael," she says, stressing your name. "Are you an adventurous man?"

You feel a chill go through you. Not a warm chill. It's the kind that scares you. Her question is loaded, and both of you know it.

"I like to think I am," you say, feigning control, feigning an adventurous spirit.

You bet she sees right through you.

"You look like you're two seconds away from sprinting out of here."

"I'm fine right where I am," you say, doing your best at acting cool.

"Do you know that the other day I saw George Clooney on that very sidewalk? Probably in town doing press for a new movie."

"You probably get a lot of that around here."

"I'm not often starstruck. In fact, I never am. But George. He's in a different class."

"Would you approach him?"

A hint of playfulness flickers in her eyes. "No. But I'd do my best to try to get him to come up to me."

"So what does that make me?"

She laughs. "A very lucky man."

"Probably," you say, your eyes locking onto hers and, for a brief second, sharing something unspoken but powerful. "So what do you do for a living?"

"Lots of things."

"Lots of jobs?"

She smiles. "I own my own business, among other things."

"Impressive."

"Not really, but I'll take it."

"What sort of business?"

"A little bit of everything."

You don't mind her vagueness. Maybe she has wealthy parents. From the look of her, she has money, wherever she's getting it from. She wears a thin watch with diamonds around its face. A small necklace with a diamond pendant dangles from her neck. There is a ring on her right hand that looks pricey.

"So have you enjoyed your time in New York?"

"You sound like a travel agent," you say.

"And you sound nervous. It's just a question."

"Actually, it's been pretty lousy, to be honest."

"How so?"

Where do I begin?

"Just work."

She looks, waits for something more. You're not about to get into it here and now with this stranger.

"I came here hoping for more. Things just—they didn't work out."

"But you're here now."

"Yes, I am."

"Things can still work out for you."

She smiles. Once again, you feel a slow-growing sense of alarm.

You take a sip from your glass. But it doesn't help.

Your fears (and part of you wonders what exactly you're afraid of) eventually subside when the unnamed woman says she must go.

"Thanks for the chat."

"You're—welcome."

"Don't worry. I've already paid for my wine."

"It's fine," you say.

She looks at you as if she's contemplating something, sizing you up.

It is not a safe look. Nothing about it is safe. It's dangerous.

"You have a pen and a business card?" she asks.

You find them and give them to her, surprised, wanting to know where this will lead.

She quickly writes down something and gives you back the card and the pen.

"Perhaps we can share another glass of wine later. If you're not too busy."

She stands, and of course you can't help but look at her. She doesn't even say good-bye and maybe that's the whole point. She's left you with a name and a phone number and now she's turned and walking away and she's leaving you with a great view. You briefly lose yourself in watching.

What just happened, and how did it happen to me?

You're not the kind of guy who gets a "Jasmine" to write out her number for you.

And you're not the guy who calls that number, for whatever reason. Whether it's to sample a serious vintage or to get yourself in serious trouble.

You're not that sort of man, despite the fact that your plane leaves in sixteen hours and you have nothing else to do and you have *a lot* of time to kill.

Because if you *were* that sort of man, there would have to be some serious reasons why, right? And you're a good guy. With a good family. And a good life.

You're not going to do anything with that number.

But you slide it into your shirt pocket anyway.

6:15 P.M.

THERE'S ANONYMITY IN NEW YORK CITY.

Even God can't keep track of everyone in this city, you think. There's so much compressed into such a small space.

You are used to Chicago, living in the suburbs and working in the city. Chicago has character; New York has crowds. Something about the faces passing you by makes you feel small and insignificant. One of the millions. Still wearing a suit you were going to wear to dinner tonight. Still wearing the new tie Lisa bought you.

There is a never-ending soundtrack of traffic and voices and life playing out around you. A myriad of colors shifting and waving. The smell of the hot dog vendor's wares almost makes you stop but you see a disaster waiting to happen smeared all over your coat. You think back to the blonde, the long legs, the phone number.

No way.

Of course you think this. Of course you won't dial it. There's some sort of catch and you're not taking it.

Maybe she's just like you. Alone in a city looking for company.

And she wants you to think this. Just like the guys you pass who want you to spend twenty-five dollars on a wallet that cost them fifty cents to make. It's part of the scenery, part of the street, part of New York.

If you're not too busy.

And you wonder how you're going to spend the night. There's nothing to do, nowhere to go, no one to see.

A man could get lost in a city like this and nobody would know. Nobody would care.

God himself might not even care.

6:37 P.M.

YOU'VE REPLAYED THE CONVERSATION in your head a dozen times, trying to see if you could have said something else or managed the situation any better.

"We've decided the markets are too volatile to go ahead with the merger at this time."

The pasty-faced guy sitting across from you wears a suit too expensive for somebody who looks as disheveled as he does and wears too much authority for someone as clueless as he acts.

"We've spoken about this for six months, Geoffrey," you say, not only stating the truth but reminding him why you're here.

You've spent six months on this project.

An entire company depends on your actions right here and now.

"I'm sorry, Mike. I mean, man, it sucks. I know. I was talking to the board yesterday. Sorry—I could've saved you a trip to the city, you know. It just—it's not going to work out."

"So what am I supposed to tell the guys back home?"

"These things aren't fail proof, Mike. They happen. It's big business. We're not a small firm like you guys. We buy and sell every day."

Three other suits, two men and a woman, stare at you with uncompromising, uncaring glances as Geoffrey talks.

"We have to be able to figure this out."

"It's not our decision to figure out. Not when there is so much money on the table."

$250,000,000 to be exact.

"I can refigure the figures. We can do that right now."

"There's no refiguring anything."

You want to take Geoffrey's chubby cheeks in your hands and rub his face in the contract. The contract you spent a couple weeks working on.

"Okay, let's just go over the final tabs one more time. Just one more time."

"I understand your anxiety, Mike," he says with a smug look that says he surely *doesn't* understand. "I know there are lots of jobs on the line here. There is a company you're looking after, and I admire that. But DB Solutions will find another buyer. We're confident of that."

You're not. You're so desperate you resort to clichés.

"Then how about if we think outside the box?"

That statement seems to annoy Geoffrey, as if people before in his life have told him the very same thing.

When someone is in a position of power like Geoffrey is, you don't talk down to him.

"Here's something outside the box. Liam spends every day of his life thinking outside the box. And he'll wake up going on his gut and his instincts. And the other day, his gut told him not to move ahead with this deal. And despite anything we do or however far we can think *outside the box*, there is no changing Liam's call. This is his deal, and if he says no, he means no."

You look at Geoffrey and know that he's being brutally honest.

"I've worked with him long enough to know," he says with a finality that stings.

You are speechless and want to say something or do something but you can't. You know it's over. You have to go back and tell a company of over 250 employees that the deal went south and they might not have a job in a few weeks.

"I'm sorry, Mike," Geoffrey says.

Yeah, I am too.

Four hours later, you look at the contract and the proposal sitting on the desk in your room at the Marriott. If you looked outside your window, you could see Times Square below. But all you want to do now is tear up these pieces of paper that are now meaningless and crawl under the sheets and try to wipe out this day and this memory from your mind.

Nothing's going to do that, however. Nothing.

Perhaps we can share another glass of wine later. If you're not too busy.

The blonde's words whisper in your ear.

Maybe they can take the agony of this defeating day away.

7:34 P.M.

YOU'RE WAITING FOR SOMEONE to pick up at home as you sit on the edge of the made bed, the room service tray right in front of you. A wet stain from the ketchup you spilled and tried to clean up looks like it's never going to dry. ESPN is talking about baseball, which doesn't really interest you. Baseball seasons take so long. Football seasons feel too short.

You hear your voice on the other end and decide to leave a message.

"Hey, Lisa—just wanted to call. Sorry I missed you earlier. You're probably at your parents'—I'll try back in a little while. Love you."

You feel a tinge of guilt.

I didn't go up to that woman. I was sitting there minding my business when she came up to me.

But you didn't answer your cell phone.

I didn't feel it vibrating.

The room feels silent and lonely.

You look at the coins and pen and key card on the desk. Next to them sits the name and the number that seem to glow in the dark.

Jasmine.

Is that even a real name?

Your cell phone sits on the bed. Ready. Waiting.

For a minute you just stare at the name, the handwriting.

A minute turns to ten, maybe twenty. You're not sure. You don't really know what you're thinking. You can blink and see the woman's face, her eyes on yours, her smile.

A beautiful woman is God's gift to man. She knows it and he knows it and there is nothing a man can do but admit it. He's weak and under her control.

You memorize the numbers. They're just numbers. It's just a name. A stranger crossing your path, never to see you again.

Ten numbers. It could be an apartment or a condo or a hotel or a cell phone.

A ring jerks you from your trance. You pick up the hotel phone.

"Mike?"

"Yeah."

"I was expecting voice mail," says your associate.

"I'm live in the flesh," you say.

"What are you doing in your hotel room?"

"Finishing off a really bad burger."

"Sad."

Barry's voice sounds too amiable.

"Where are you?" you ask.

"Just got back to O'Hare."

"Why didn't you take me with you?"

"Just got your message. Are you serious?"

"I wish I wasn't."

He curses. "That totally sucks."

"Yeah."

"What are you going to tell Connelly?"

"The truth. What else can I say?"

"It's officially off?"

"I tried everything. They're done."

"Do you know why?"

"Maybe you should have stuck around. Bailed me out of this."

"Yeah, right," Barry says. "I probably would have freaked out on them."

"It's numbers. It's all about numbers. Too many people on their end, not enough profit on ours."

You want to say more but can't. A sick feeling is forming in your gut.

"You couldn't get a flight out?"

"Didn't even try."

"Look—you're in Manhattan. It's a Friday night. And you're what? Watching *Law and Order*?"

"ESPN."

"Harsh. They'll be showing the same stuff in eight hours. Go out. Do something. Anything."

"Thanks, Dad."

"I'd take you out if I was there. If you were a going-out sort of guy."

"I go out. I just don't black out like you."

"Funny. Come on. You deserve a few drinks after a day like today."

"Who said I didn't already have a few?"

"Okay, then have a few more. Take your mind off things."

"Don't ever go into counseling," you say with a laugh.

"Yeah, well, I might have to after today. You know? Hey—I gotta get my luggage. Call me when you get back to Chicago."

"Sure."

"And Mike. Man—don't dwell on it. It wasn't your fault."

"Who said it was?"

"Connelly will."

"Yeah, right."

He laughs.

You hear the phone click and you just hold it in your hands. You'd like to throw it or at least bash it over someone's head. Maybe your own.

The line goes dead and you hang up.

And the numbers draw you in.

You look back at the handwritten note. Very pretty hand-writing.

You pick up your cell phone.

Without thought, you punch each number.

One. After another. After another.

And then you hear the ring.

You don't really want to do this.

That's not true. Maybe it's more like you really *shouldn't* do this.

But you stay on. And on the fourth ring, on what should be voice mail, on what should be you hanging up and tearing up the business card and waiting for your wife to call, you hear her voice.

"It took you long enough," she says.

You feel a head rush and can't say anything for few seconds. Does she know it's you calling?

"I haven't given my number to anyone else, Chicago boy."

And you suddenly realize that this might not be a con, or an indecent proposal, or anything other than a stranger like you in a strange land.

"I didn't expect to get you."

The laugh she gives is gentle and friendly. "I'm here. For now."

You can't speak. You have no idea what to say.

"You were more talkative in person."

"Yeah."

"So I'll make this easy."

Here it comes.

"I'm heading over to Atmosphere. A great lounge in the Village. I'm sure you can find a cab to take you there."

"Probably."

Again, you hear her laugh. Not mocking. More playful, like she finds this shy childhood conversation amusing.

"And I'll be with several friends, so don't worry."

"About what?"

"I won't bite."

And before you can say anything, she hangs up.

Again, you're left with the phone in your hand.

Your forehead feels sweaty, but the air conditioner is cranked. You go over to the windows and open the drapes, revealing a New York just ready to turn on.

Go on out, a voice tells you.

You deserve a drink.

Make something out of this abysmal failure.

You hear Barry's voice. *Okay, then have a few more. Take your mind off things.*

Besides, she'll be with several friends.

There's nothing wrong with going out and having a conversation and enjoying yourself. Nothing at all.

You go near the window and stare out at the city and the

activity and you feel lonely and you hate being all alone. There's something about the silence, even with white noise around you, that feels hollow. That feels threatening.

You don't do well alone.

Tonight, you're not going to be.

8:07 P.M.

PERHAPS IT'S THE CITY, the seeming endlessness of the Big Apple.

Perhaps it's the end of a long month, or a bleak end to a long account, a quick conclusion to a long conflict.

Perhaps it's the fact that you and Lisa haven't been communicating well lately and that the children have been more of the focus than the two of you. You can't communicate when a thousand other details drain and bombard you on a daily basis.

Perhaps it's the fact that your mom is slowly dying of a fast-moving disease. You have seen and heard about it, but when it lands on your doorstep with its dementia and delusions, there is nothing you can do. Nothing. And when you have to explain to your mother, an only child to his only parent, that she is indeed your mother, it tends to weigh you down.

But all the *perhapses* in the world can't fully explain this restless feeling that walks the sidewalk with you.

Sometimes you feel like the world is passing you by. There is a better world out there and you're not in it. There is always someone younger and wealthier and happier. Someone more beautiful and sexy and witty to be with. A more put-together snapshot that should go out at Christmastime to hundreds of your close friends.

It's the myth and the lie but sometimes you bite on it and get caught in the hook.

A billboard shows you the results of a new diet pill. In fact, it shows you three results, women all tanned and toned and sweaty in their bathing suits barely there. The billboard is as big as your house.

Another advertisement shows a lingerie model in a black outfit that would make Lisa laugh and roll her eyes and say, "In your dreams."

Dreams. Yes, in your dreams.

It's easy to be restless.

Sure, you can look away. You're not going to gawk in the middle of Times Square.

But it's not just that.

This restless feeling is a culmination of many things.

The business trip. You get your morning paper, see five

men's magazines with the latest blonde or brunette doing her best to look sexy in a provocative pose and outfit. You never buy those magazines, not even the tamer ones that try to offer other variations of themes like sports and "men's topics." You'd be embarrassed to buy a magazine like that. But sometimes, every now and then, you pick one up and look. It's nothing too blatant or perverse. But it's enough. The images stick with you.

And then you'll be on a plane. In a city. In a restaurant or a hotel. In a meeting or waiting room. And an attractive woman can come out of nowhere. Sometimes just cute, sometimes alluring. And you feel a slight pull, a tiny tug.

This is the restlessness you feel. The feeling that you can't look, you can't touch, you can't act. You know this and you accept it, but sometimes it's hard.

It's the city and your mind and the fear of things.

Yeah. The fear of things.

What are you afraid of, Mike? What are you really afraid of?

You wonder again if you're alone and anonymous and if your actions and mind can be seen from the heavens above.

God doesn't care about your doubts and fears, does he?

If he doesn't care about things like a job and a family, why would he concern himself with something like the random thoughts of a restless mind?

There are ways to make this restless feeling go away. Temporarily, yes, sure. But sometimes something temporary and fleeting and passing is better than nothing at all.

8:34 P.M.

VELVET WALLS LINE THE THIN HALLWAY. A steady, heavy beat moves with you, not fast enough to dance to but not slow enough to be just background. The main room is cozy with a packed, ornate bar and beds that pose for couches around small, modern tables. There are still a few empty chairs and places at the bar. Your first sweep of the room doesn't find her, so you decide to get a drink and play it cool.

Someone might find out that you don't belong. That doesn't prevent you from ordering a gin and tonic, or leaning against the bar for a moment, or casually glancing around the glimmering lounge. Then you spot her; she sits on a loveseat by herself, across from a redheaded woman leaning over the table and talking nonstop with her hands waving over their drinks. She sees you but doesn't smile or wave or acknowledge you. Instead she looks back at her friend, who keeps talking. Then she looks your way and motions you over.

You feel like such a little kid.

"You decided to venture out," she says with a smile.

"Why not?"

"I like the jeans. Big improvement over the tie."

A thought automatically runs through your mind, something about how stunning she looks. You keep it to yourself. She is wearing a different outfit, a short khaki skirt with a black off-the-shoulder top and tall black boots. The sight of her takes your breath away, literally, because you know you're not only talking to her but that she asked you to come here and be with her.

"You should have let me get that for you," she says, glancing at the drink in your hand. "We've got a tab."

Her friend is an attractive, round-faced woman with expressive eyes that look friendly.

"This is Amanda," Jasmine says.

"Here, have a seat," Amanda says, urging you to take her place.

"No, that's okay—"

"No, really, it's fine. I was just telling her I had to take off."

"You really don't have—"

"Give me a call later, okay?" Amanda asks.

She strides away, and you sit down awkwardly.

"Am I interrupting?"

Jasmine looks after Amanda and shakes her head.

"We were just chatting. She might be back later. It's early for New York."

"I thought you said you'd be with friends."

"I was. And more may be coming. This place is home anyway. I know the owner."

The table between the two of you is small with three burning candles in the middle. You sit on a round chair that resembles an ottoman while Jasmine sinks back into her loveseat. For a second she glances at you and you feel a wave of chills wash over you. She's probably used to doing that, affecting men that way.

"No more wine?" she asks as she gently rubs one of her crossed legs.

"I figured I'd be a little more adventurous."

"That's really stretching yourself," she says with her red lips curling in a grin.

Being here is really stretching myself.

"Still drinking wine?" you say to continue the conversation.

"For now. Sometimes I get in different moods, you know. I get tired of the same old thing. That's my motto. Tired of the same old thing."

"I can relate."

She studies you for a second.

"So what bores you the most?" she asks.

"About what?"

"About your life?"

Monday morning meetings with the VPs.

It's scary how quickly your mind answered her question.

"Boring meetings at work."

"You know what it is for me? Small talk. Chitchat." She curses, and the word coming so casually from such a beautiful woman surprises you. "Everybody has things they *really* want to say, but never say them. You know?"

You nod and feel an anxiousness rising in your gut.

"For instance, I could try and say something about Amanda leaving, but frankly, I wanted her to go. I asked her to leave when you got here. And I think, if you were going to be honest, you'd tell me you're glad that she left."

"She didn't have to—"

"You didn't come out tonight to meet my friends," Jasmine says. "See, there is polite chitchat. What you were about to say. Which is nice and polite. But tell me something, Michael. What did you really think when you first got here?"

How hot you look.

You open your mouth but nothing comes out.

Jasmine laughs. She knows what you're thinking.

"Okay, let me ask you another question. What's the most adventurous thing you've ever done?" She asks as though you've been friends for half a dozen years.

You think of your children. Olivia and Peyton. Deciding to venture into fatherhood is by far the boldest and craziest thing you've ever done, but you're not going to tell her that. You don't want to mention them, nor do you want to say the name Lisa. Why complicate things?

And by the way, why'd you leave your ring back in your hotel room?

"I spent a couple weeks in India," you say.

But you don't mention it was on a missions trip after college. No need to let her know this. She doesn't look like the church sort of girl anyway. Leaving out this bit of information is sort of like not wearing your wedding ring.

"Let me rephrase the question. What's the *craziest* thing you've ever done?"

"Crazy as in?"

"As in insane. As in breathtaking. Exhilarating. Intoxicating."

She gently licks her lips, and you can't help but stare at her for a moment. This can't be happening. Something is wrong with this picture. A woman like her usually doesn't look back and smile and talk to you. She usually is unmovable and touched up behind the pages of a magazine or on a Web site. The seductive glance is for show, for the camera, for the allure of the picture and the enticement of the customer.

Am I a customer?

She picks up on the silence and continues. "I once went streaking in Times Square."

"I had some streaking moments in college."

"Times Square," she repeats.

"You just decided to run naked through Midtown?"

She laughs. "The cops grabbed me and put a coat over me. They let me go. One tried to ask me out on a date."

"You win. That trumps anything I've ever done."

"Don't you ever want to just abandon all reason and go where the spirit leads?"

Maybe that's what I'm doing now.

"I don't think my spirit would lead me to streak in front of several thousand strangers."

"I didn't see anybody complaining."

She smiles, perfect lips parting to reveal perfect teeth. Nothing about her looks fake—just nearly flawless.

You finish your drink and know you need another. Because if you seriously think about what you're doing talking with this woman, you'll start second-guessing yourself. Instead, you want something—you need something—to coat over your conscience like the ceaseless, seductive beats and orange glow that cover you.

8:54 P.M.

YOU HAVE ALWAYS HAD A WEAKNESS for a pretty face. Some might say that all guys are the same, that they're all pigs, that they only want one thing. But you're not like that. You're not one of them. But you do have a weakness for something alluring, something appealing, something that takes you off guard and that makes your mind and your heart stop.

You can remember the first time you met Lisa. She stopped you even though you pretended not to notice her and kept walking and kept looking ahead and kept talking.

A younger man in an easier world. That was the setting and the climate. College and classes and dreams of a bigger and better world.

God if I could just go back just for a second just for a moment.

When a kiss was the only thing you wanted. When the

cares of a hundred other causes and responsibilities didn't rule your world.

You passed her on a college sidewalk. She was like a ladybird settling by, glancing, then flying off.

She was a science major and you were a business major and she might have been one of a hundred other cute girls that captivated your mind. But something about her was different, stood out, got your heart and your head thinking and spinning.

You were a sophomore and she was a junior.

You came from Denver, Colorado, and she came from Schaumburg, Illinois.

She had a boyfriend and you were just coming off a bad relationship.

Things have a way of working out, don't they? The map of a relationship and a love is never easy to navigate, never predictable, never easy to track. But somehow that single passing on a sidewalk signaled a different path you'd take.

Brown eyes that conquered your heart and soul.

Enough to make you start asking questions about who she was and where she hung out. Enough to get you to pass by her again, to finally stop and talk with her, to get to know her.

And so many years later, you're staring at different eyes, and you have a tinge of guilt because you know they're not the eyes you should be looking at. These are not the eyes that should be moving you. And no matter how much you drink or think or rationalize or bury or disregard, you know that those eyes don't belong to you and can never belong to you.

And any sane man would run far away.

This isn't a sweet college student on a sidewalk in North Carolina who has suddenly captured your attention.

And this can never be a sweet memory you'll think of with fondness a decade from now.

9:14 P.M.

"YOU HAVE NICE HANDS."

Jasmine's comment surprises you. For a second you look at her to see if she is joking.

"Really?"

"Sure."

"I've never thought of my hands as 'nice.' "

"They're hot."

You laugh now, thinking she's making fun of you. "Come on."

"No, I'm serious. Hands are a big deal to me. And the thing I always check out on men—their forearms."

You're looking at your hands and forearms as if it's the first time you've ever studied them. In fact, it might be.

"Some guys—they have flabby hands and forearms. Like baby fat or something. You don't. Yours are very nice."

The smile on your lips can't go away now. Even if she's just playing with your mind, she's doing a great job at it. Have a drink and hear a compliment, and boy, does it do wonders for the spirit.

Her long, slender hands touch yours, first caressing your palm, then feeling your wrist and forearm.

"You have strong hands, very sexy."

"Thank you," you say.

This is crazy.

You want to return the compliment, but everything that comes to mind seems inappropriate.

Is it bad to compliment a beautiful woman and just tell her the truth?

You don't want to think what's right and what's wrong.

"So what's your favorite part on a woman?"

You inhale and laugh.

"Come on. It can be anything. It doesn't have to be the thing most guys would say. Be creative."

"I like a lot of things."

"Okay."

"I mean, the first thing I noticed about you—when you first sat down, I couldn't help but notice—you know, when you crossed your legs . . ."

Jasmine's smile fills her face, and her eyes light up. "You're a leg man."

"Sure, yeah, I guess."

She nods.

"That wasn't very creative," you say.

"But it was true, right?"

"Sure."

She's studying you again, looking your way with eyes that seem curious and amused.

"What are you thinking?" you ask.

"How old are you?"

You let out a chuckle. "How old do I look?"

"I don't know. Maybe, let's see—midthirties. Right?"

"Thirty-seven."

You don't mind her knowing your age. You have never felt like a thirty-something to begin with. The number revealed on your driver's license doesn't designate how old you feel or act.

"You want to guess my age?" she asks.

"I don't want to be rude."

"Give me a break. It's fun."

"Twenty-five," you say, a general round number for an age.

"Close. Twenty-six."

You're glad to hear she didn't say twenty-one. She still looks younger than she really is.

"Okay, so look, Michael. Here's the deal. If you have a thought, any thought, tonight, tell me. Tell me at that very moment. Okay?"

"Sure."

She laughs. "You say that *so* unconvincingly. You need to relax. Come on. I swear I'm not going to hurt you. Just—I know there are thoughts you're not saying. Maybe it takes you a little time to warm up."

"This isn't something I'm particularly used to."

"Then I'm giving you a golden opportunity tonight. Let me teach you."

Teach me what?

Once again she takes your hand in both of her own. "You're so cute, you know that?"

It's been a while since another woman called you cute. Since your hand was held deliberately and not as an after-thought, as if someone wanted to hold it, as if it meant something to them.

You feel a soft, slow tingle begin to smolder deep below.

Maybe it's the booze. You've ordered a few drinks and have lost track.

That's not really it, is it?

Her touch, her eyes, her lips, her hair, almost everything about her . . .

That's what's doing this. What's causing this.

You're beginning to really lose yourself.

You can't help it.

"Relax," Jasmine says. "Everything will be fine."

9:29 P.M.

You're not very good at relaxing.

You can't remember the last time you took a vacation.

You always have to be doing something. Anything.

In the morning you take out the dog. He's Lisa's dog and makes that clear. He's a Lhasa Apso and seems a little annoyed at your existence but still relies on you to take him out to do his morning duty.

You make your coffee and your quick breakfast and you read the paper. You find yourself interested in items that have absolutely nothing to do with your life. But you read with fascination about politics and finances and sports teams and the box office reports and the star news and the latest gadgets and the local Chicago news.

It takes you about an hour to get to work, forty-five

minutes if you're lucky or early, an hour and a half on bad days. You listen to talk radio and find others' opinions on things fascinating. You've grown used to the voices and the programs and find them more interesting than most other things in your life.

There are the people you work with and deal with and pass by and share life's anecdotes with.

Then there is the work, for which you take a chunk of your life and break it up and scatter it around like pieces of bread for birds.

You've been working on this merger for over half a year.

Late nights and weekends have been devoted to plans and numbers and options and opportunities.

All swirling around the ceramic toilet bowl of emptiness. Going to a sewer of nothingness.

You wanted this deal—strike that, you *needed* this deal— and you busted your butt to make it happen.

And on the faith front, well, things haven't been particularly exemplary. If faith were a class, you'd be getting a solid D.

Come on, God. Give me a break down here. Give me a little help. Can't you? I'm not asking for much and I never ask for much and I do my own thing day after day putting in time and putting in energy and this is what I get?

Sometimes you wonder if you should expect anything. If you deserve anything.

Sometimes you deserve something. Don't you? For all the

hard work and the emotional energy and the busyness of life, don't you sometimes deserve to take a break and just have a little fun?

9:48 P.M.

NO FRIENDS. NO LAST NAME. No profession or even personal information. The past hour has been spent talking about the most trivial of topics: types of vodka, expensive shoes, a woman she sees and knows and can't stand, music. But in the midst of the small talk, Jasmine throws out boldly personal questions without blinking. After finishing her third martini, she excuses herself. You sit and wait and after fifteen minutes you begin to wonder if the conversation and your fear of opening up got to her.

The place is getting more crowded. So many twenty- and thirty-somethings with their lean figures and expensive clothes and smiles and conversations. You try to remember the last time you were at a place like this. When was the last time you were out at all besides for a work function? Most of going out for work means steak dinners and an occasional drink afterwards, but not to some hip and trendy place like this. You wonder what Lisa would think of it.

You look around and know that if you step away from the table, someone else will grab it. But you continue to wait and she doesn't come back. You stand and look for her, but a sea of heads and faces engulf you.

I'm not waiting around like a fool.

You take your half-empty drink and head to the restrooms, down the velvet hallway and through a side corridor. You pass a small room on your right and don't look inside but hear her voice.

"—could say anything and you'd still act the same—"

And then you hear a male voice interrupting.

"Sit back down."

"No."

"I swear, don't do this. Not now. Just sit back down."

The voice sounds angry and threatening. You turn and look into the room. All you see is the back of a man leaning over someone on a couch. For a second you stand in the doorway. You see the long suede boots belonging to Jasmine. Her long legs look uncomfortable, as if shielding her from the man who stands over her.

"Everything okay in here?" you call out.

A man with glassy, fiery eyes and short, curly hair turns

and looks at you. He's wearing a dress shirt with several buttons undone and black pants.

"Did anybody ask you?"

He's not a big guy; you're probably taller and broader. But the look on his face says enough, and if you were a stranger encountering this—whatever this is—you'd move on. But Jasmine looks concerned, maybe even upset.

Is she crying?

"You okay?" you ask her.

She nods and then looks down. The guy curses at you and tells you to take a hike.

"Why don't you back away from the lady?"

"If there's a lady in this room I'll back away from her."

"Jasmine—"

The stranger looks at you, then at the blonde, then back at you. He cackles and then appears amused.

"Jasmine? Sorry, buddy, you got the wrong *lady.*"

"Riley, please," says Jasmine.

Or whatever her name is.

"Are you okay?" you ask her.

This time, she only looks your way.

The man walks toward you and gets in your face. "This isn't your concern."

"Maybe she wants to leave."

"Maybe I don't care."

Jasmine stands up and walks behind the man. In her heels

she's a couple inches taller than he is. He snatches her arm, pulling her down to the ground. Pulling her down violently.

She lets out a muffled shriek.

Maybe it's the gin or the adrenaline or something else flowing in you. This man touching Jasmine—no, make that grabbing her and pulling her down—doesn't fly with you. You grab his shoulder, pulling him toward you and getting him off balance. He releases Jasmine's arm just a little, enough for her to jerk it away from him and then dash past you.

"Oh, man," he starts in on you, shocked that you actually touched him. He launches a couple curses at you.

"Leave her alone."

"Who let you in to begin with? You'll never step foot in this place again."

Jasmine has left the room and you try to follow when the man shoves you from behind. You're propelled toward one of the hallway walls and slam up against it. You hear a few more juicy expletives behind you.

"This is *so* not your problem, man," he says as he walks up to you.

A couple approaching the scene in the hallway stop and look on. You look at the man, now standing ready to go in front of the doorway. Then you start to walk toward Jasmine, past the curious couple and out of this place.

As the couple hurry past, you feel a hand grip your shirt and pull you back.

You turn and grab his hand, forcing it to let go of your shirt. Then you punch him hard, squarely on the nose. This isn't the first time you've punched somebody and made it hurt. Knuckles landing that hard on the cartilage of the nose do damage.

The man wails in pain and slumps over, going to his knees and cursing. You don't bother to look at him any longer. You walk away and find Jasmine outside the lounge, standing against the side of the building lighting up a cigarette.

"What was that all about?" you ask.

"I'm so sorry."

You rub your throbbing hand as she looks at you.

"What happened?" she asks.

"Nothing," you say. "Who was that guy?"

"He's the owner."

You watch her smoke her cigarette in earnest. "Guess I won't be coming back here."

"What'd you do to him?"

"Just made sure he wouldn't touch you again."

"You don't know him," she says, a look of fear on her face.

"Let's get out of here."

You walk down the sidewalk and try to find an intersection with a cab. Your hand hurts more than you thought it would. You wonder how the guy's nose feels.

"Did you hurt him?" Jasmine asks.

"Yeah."

"Good."

"How do you know him?"

A cab pulls up. You open the door for her. She takes one last drag from her cigarette and then flicks it away.

"He's my ex. Long story. Very long story."

I'm not going anywhere.

You follow her into the cab and see her skirt slide up her thigh and you feel more alive than you have for a very long time.

10:43 P.M.

THE STREETS SEEM EVERLASTING, the strangers you pass seem endless. There is an energy on these streets that doesn't exist anywhere else, an attitude that could only be successfully carried off in New York. The taxi flies through the neighborhood and around turns and you hold the door handle as you look over at the profile of Jasmine's face. She seems to have regained her composure.

"Tell me something."

"Yeah."

"Is your name really Jasmine?"

She stares at you for a moment, fearless eyes that look amused. "Does it matter?"

"I guess not."

"I can show you my license. But really—what'd be the point?"

Your head feels light from the drinks. The cab jerks and turns down a side street.

"Where are we going?"

Jasmine grins. "I don't recall inviting you anywhere."

"Oh, sure—yeah. I just thought it would be best to get out of there."

"Look, *Michael*, or whatever your name is. You look tense."

You looked tense a few minutes ago.

"I just tried to break some guy's nose."

"Great feeling, huh?"

"I'm not sure what sort of feeling I should have."

"If you knew Riley, you'd understand."

"Understand what?"

"Some men are just—they're not good guys. You're a good guy. I could tell that the moment I walked up to you at Rockefeller Center. Riley, unfortunately, is not one of those."

"You dated him?"

"I didn't know he was a bad guy."

"Bad, meaning—?"

"Bad. Abusive bad. Out-of-control bad. Scary bad."

You nod and notice that she seems to be revealing a sense of alarm as she glances out the window.

"You okay?"

"Of course," she says, the confidence there again, her tone suggesting she is always okay.

You think of Riley. There's nothing you can stand less

than a guy who hurts women. You find yourself wishing you'd broken a few other things as well.

"We shouldn't have gone there in the first place," Jasmine says. "I thought he wouldn't be there."

"Do you want to go home?"

"Are you crazy?" She laughs. "Do you?"

"No, I'm fine."

She puts a hand on your leg and gently rubs it. "You need to relax. The night is young."

"My flight leaves at 9:00 a.m."

"A lot can happen by then." She smiles. "Come on—I want to show you the city."

11:00 P.M.

A PICTURE MUCH BRIGHTER POPS INTO YOUR MIND.

But sometimes the brightness of the day doesn't match the mood in your heart.

You're sitting on the deck of the cottage overlooking the Atlantic. It is midday after a particularly disastrous night. You have a cup of coffee and look out onto the ocean. A thousand golden flickers streak throughout the ever-moving waters, a steady coating over the earth that seems to go on forever.

Does anything go on forever? you wonder.

Everything comes to an end.

You hear her behind you but don't look as she comes onto the porch and sits in the chair next to you.

"So what now?" she asks.

You don't know. You have no clue. This vacation has

turned into a nightmare. A change of scenery doesn't always repair the wounds that have been inflicted but never addressed in many years of marriage.

"I'm not sure," you say weakly.

"I'm sorry about last night."

"It doesn't change what was said."

"I didn't mean it."

"Yes, you did," you tell her. "You always mean what you say."

"I was angry, and I'm sorry."

The soft coating sound of the ocean calms you but doesn't offer hope or explanation.

For the first time since you've been married, you're wondering if it's worth going on.

"What are you thinking?" Lisa asks.

"I don't really know."

But that's mostly false. You know. But you're too scared to admit it. You hate failures, and this is a colossal failure. Seven years and it's resulted in this. Even a trip to the outer banks of North Carolina can't solve the problem.

"We need to talk to someone," she says.

"Who?"

"I don't know. It's just—we can't keep going like this."

"I know that."

"I'm sorry."

You nod. You wish you could hold Lisa in your arms and

feel alive and electric and brand new and feel like this would be eternal and that nothing or nobody would ever change it. You used to be able to do that. But life moves on. Schedules fill and disappointments arise and compromises suffice and you find yourself on the shores of the ocean wondering if you can continue living with this woman.

When did I fall out of love with her?

The things she said last night about your job and your workaholic tendencies and your bad habits and all of that—sure, they were harsh and didn't go down well. But they were true. You both knew it.

A man who would rather spend time surfing the web to find fulfillment than be with his wife—yeah, sure, that man has a problem. But problems can be handled and this is one that can be fixed.

It can't end like this. Other couples end like this but not you.

You want to pray and maybe you should pray but God hasn't been hearing those prayers so you wonder why you should keep hurling them up at him.

You sigh.

"Things can change," she says.

"How?"

"I don't know. I can stop working. We can start a family. We can move. I don't know."

All that will do is patch up a sore that's not going to heal. Put a Band-Aid on a wound that needs to be lanced.

I'm not going down without a fight.

This isn't over. Not now and not like this.

"Let's talk with someone," you say.

It's the first time you've admitted that no, your marriage isn't perfect. That yes, you need a little help. That no, you can't do it on your own.

This memory is five years old. Since then Olivia and Peyton have both been born. Lisa has stopped working and you've managed to control some of your late-night vices. For the most part.

Things should be fine, right?

You wonder if you've learned anything in all that time.

Is the problem your marriage?

Or is the problem you?

11:04 P.M.

A MAN STANDS OUTSIDE THE OPEN DOOR looking around without expression. A couple stand nearby smoking and laughing. Jasmine nods at the guy and moves one of the heavy black curtains that rest in front of the doorway. You follow her into muted color and funky vibes.

A bar is thronged with well-dressed bodies and happy faces that pay attention to Jasmine but ignore you. Broad cushioned couches line the wall, and candles make the mood. You pass the crowd and enter through another curtain down a corridor to an open room with romantically lit alcoves. Jasmine has been here before. She leads you into a section snuggled away from the main floor and sinks back into a comfortable couch and motions for you to sit next to her.

"I won't bite," she says for the second time.

This is a dream and it's not happening. It can't be. You rest on the couch and feel Jasmine shift toward you. The bass throbs and your mind feels dizzy and you know you really need a drink.

What would Lisa think?

You think of the cheesy little saying you've seen on wrists and bumper stickers. *What would Jesus do?*

Chances are Lisa wouldn't be happy and Jesus wouldn't be here.

And you don't know why you're thinking of either of them. Why can't you have a night off not to worry or feel pressure? Why can't you simply have fun with a strange and beautiful woman knowing nothing is going to happen?

I'm safe and nothing is going to happen.

The waitress comes and Jasmine orders for you. She's your guide into this night and you wonder where she's going to take you.

I've never spent time with a woman this attractive.

She doesn't seem to mind the silence. You're immersed in the music, which both relaxes and hypnotizes you. It makes you feel free, just like the alcohol does and will. Perhaps they are the perfect temporary solution for the busyness and emptiness of the working day. It might almost work.

Almost.

"What do you think of this place?"

"Very funky," you reply.

The waiter brings you the order of Long Island Iced Teas. Jasmine smiles and takes a sip and squeezes her lips together.

"They make the best Long Islands here."

You take a sip and taste first the sweetness and then the liquor inside. It's strong and warms you as it goes down.

"Like it?"

You nod.

"That'll make you relax a little more."

"Why do you keep saying that?"

"What?"

"About being more relaxed?"

"Your body says more than your mouth can. Your shoulders are tight. The way you rub your hands together and look around as though someone you know might be just around the corner. Your fidgetiness. The way you sometimes brush your eyebrows."

"So you don't worry about anything?"

"What's there to worry about? It's a Friday night in New York, and I feel great."

"What about Riley showing up?"

She shakes her head. "He won't come here."

Her face glows and her lips look soft and wet and you can't keep from staring at her. She takes another sip and you follow her example.

"Sometimes seeing the same people gets old, doesn't it?"

You nod.

"Every now and then I pick a perfect stranger—like you—and decide just to hang out with him."

"Always a him?"

"Sure. Sometimes. It's not like I'm picking guys up. It's just—I don't know. I have my reasons. My friends say I'm a little too easy-spirited, and sometimes that gets me in trouble. With guys like Riley, you know. But most of the time it's just fun shaking things up and getting to know someone you never would have met if you didn't take the initiative."

"Where would you be if you weren't here?"

She crosses a leg and moves closer to you. It's hard to hear so you have to talk in her ear. You smell her perfume, the scent of her hair.

"I'd be here regardless. I love 345."

"That's what this place is called? I didn't see a name on the front."

For the next few minutes, you get closer and continue to work on your drink and continue to look into her green-blue eyes. The music rolls and the lights seem to dim and you order another drink and watch Jasmine move her lips and laugh. You keep feeling more comfortable and relaxed and uncaring and everything around you is cushioning you.

You no longer look away when you're lost in Jasmine's gaze. She can read your mind and you're okay with her knowing what you're thinking. It's written all over your face.

"So what about you, Mr. Businessman-on-a-business-trip?"

"What about me?"

"Where would you be?"

You think of the image of being at home with a four-year-old and a two-year-old. Chuck E. Cheese's doesn't do candle-light or Long Island Iced Teas. You picture your finished basement that has become the play area with a thousand toys spread out over the plush carpet. Long gone are the nights when you and Lisa could simply curl up on a couch and watch a movie, or maybe do more than that. There are two constant needs that you have to care for, and while their needs are ones you'll happily oblige, sometimes you forget what it's like to sit down on a couch by yourself instead of holding Peyton or sitting on top of one of Olivia's toys.

"Somewhere very far away," you reply. "So far away, I don't want to think about it."

"Reality, huh?"

"Yeah."

"Then don't think about it. Not if you don't want to. It's fine by me."

The DNA of this woman is off, is different, is very unlike that of most of the women you know. You know Lisa's friends and the women in your small group and at your office and at your church. You see them in the neighborhood and out at dinner with a few couples or at the movies.

You've never encountered a woman like Jasmine.

She stares at you, through you. Her smile is replaced with

a deep gaze, seductive and sincere. It scares you with its desire.

"You're never going to meet someone like me," she says.

Confident, assured, in control.

Her face is close to yours. And your mind turns and twists and all you can think is one thing.

Okay, so look, Michael. Here's the deal. If you have a thought, any thought, tonight, tell me. Tell me at that very moment. Okay?

So you tell her exactly what you're thinking.

"I want to kiss you," you say.

And an amused smile crosses the lips you want to touch. She doesn't move away, but she almost seems to watch and wait to see what you're going to do.

As you're lost looking at Jasmine, your mind over-whelmed at being around her, you barely notice the man approaching your table.

He slides up on the couch next to you and smiles.

"Having a good time?"

The moment you're in pops like a floating bubble.

You can smell a shower of cologne and regardless of how it smells you know it's too much. A white grin gleams at you as his hand moves your glass. You notice the pinky ring, then the necklace, then his large, glistening watch. He's not a big guy, whoever this is. But his glance doesn't waver as he looks at you and waits for a response. You look over to Jasmine to see if she recognizes him.

"Not tonight," is all she says.

"Not tonight? Oh, I'm sorry. Am I interrupting?"

Another man, this one with shoulders that take up half the wall and a military buzz cut, sits next to Jasmine.

"What do you want?"

The guy next to you is the one doing the talking, the one that Jasmine talks to. He ignores you and looks at her. His voice is loud and can be heard clearly over the music. His hair is slicked back and greasy looking.

"We have some unfinished business."

"It's never finished with you," Jasmine says, unrattled by the men surrounding you.

"It can always be finished with me."

"Not tonight," Jasmine says.

"What's your story?" he asks you.

"No story here."

"Maybe this friendly soul can help you out."

"Clark—" Jasmine says.

"Tell me, you know this young lady?"

"I don't think it's any of your business," you say.

Amazing how a little liquor can inject bravado into your spirit.

He puts a finger in your face. "Everything is my business when I want it to be."

"Can this wait?" Jasmine asks.

"I've been waiting long enough."

"But tonight?"

"The habits of rich New York kids never stop. Tonight's as good a night as any."

"Maybe she wants some space," you say.

He looks at you and puts an arm around you.

"Who the hell are you?"

"A friend."

He nods. "Shreve has lots of friends."

You wonder if Shreve is her last name. You try not to react.

"The problem is, Shreve has *too many* friends. Too many places to go. Too many things to do. Too many opportunities to slip away. Don't you?"

"Let's go outside," Jasmine says.

"Really?"

She glares at the man she called Clark. "Yeah, really. Tell steroids here to move over."

You're about to say something when Jasmine grabs your hand. "I'm fine. I'm sorry—let me just talk with them for a few minutes."

"You sure?"

She nods and squeezes your leg to calm you down.

The heavy next to Jasmine stands up, and she and the man next to you walk away.

"I'll be right back. Swear."

You nod.

"Why don't you stay in here and order another drink?" Clark says.

Jasmine glances at you, and you see the tough, fearless look on her face has vanished. She looks like she's about to say something else, then she turns. The guys follow her through the curtain and away.

You eat the ice in your drink and when the waiter comes by you decide why not and order another.

Midnight is closing in and you're more awake than you were six hours ago and you relax on the comfortable sofa and watch the crowd around you and you feel like a different man.

There are pressures that await you that you don't want to think about. The family suburban house dog mortgage bills friends family church whole ball of wax.

You just want a little breathing room. Right now, on this sofa, in this dimly lit room packed with strangers, syncopated beats bouncing off you, your head warm and relaxed, you want to simply enjoy this. Jasmine will come back and will sit next to you and whisper in your ear and you'll enjoy glancing at those eyes and those lips and that smile and the long blonde hair and you'll think you're a different person living a different life without the heaviness and you'll enjoy it just for a moment.

Just for one moment. That's all you want.

So you wait for Jasmine to return.

And wait.

And wait.

11:42 P.M.

YOU PRESS 4 ON YOUR CELL PHONE and get your voice mail at work. You check it all the time and now that you're waiting here you decide why not.

You have one new message. From your mother.

"Michael, I was wondering if you could come over and take care of Whisper for the weekend. I'm going to be taking a business trip to California for a few days. Can you give me a call, please?"

You have to laugh. In fact, you laugh so hard your side hurts.

Sometimes all you can do is laugh. Laugh or cry, as they say.

Whisper is your mother's cat that died about ten years ago. Your mother hasn't worked in at least twenty years.

The Alzheimer's is doing a number on her.

You are used to getting voice mails like this. Or calls out of the blue. They used to freak you out before you understood what was going on. Sometimes it would make you deeply sad. But now, the only way of dealing with it and moving on is to laugh.

Dear Mom.

You'd like to think that your prayers for your mother could be answered. But now you just pray that she keeps herself out of trouble and harm's way and that the disease moves as slowly as possible.

But the writing is on the wall. You know it. Prayers aren't going to help.

Mom has always cheered you up. And even now, without intending to, she manages to make you smile.

You save the message because you'll want to play it again sometime when you're having a bad day.

MIDNIGHT

SHE'S COMING BACK.

You keep telling yourself that. You keep looking at the purse next to you that she left behind. But it's been over half an hour.

For a second, you consider leaving her purse here and going outside to see where she went. But you can't leave it here. She needs to return, and you want to make sure you don't miss her.

So you take the small, black purse and walk past the crowd at the bar. When you first stand up, your head feels light. You balance yourself and suddenly realize those Long Island Iced Teas have done a number on you.

Am I drunk?

No, of course not. You won't admit that you are, anyway.

You look around for the blonde hair but you don't see her. You make it outside and find yourself on a sidewalk with a few smoking strangers that don't look anything like Jasmine.

"You see a blonde recently?"

Smoker number one just looks at you, while smoker number two shakes his head. The big guy who doesn't need to be wearing his leather coat stares straight ahead, either deaf or oblivious.

"You see a blonde come out here? With a couple of guys?"

"I see a lot of blondes."

"Good-looking. Tall. Skirt and boots."

"Yeah, sure."

You wait for more, but he looks at a couple passing into the lounge.

"Any idea where they went?"

He looks annoyed, but you don't back down. Amazing how *a lot* of liquor can inspire confidence.

Or stupidity.

"Got in a car and left."

"A cab? Car? What?"

"A car. It was waiting."

You think about asking him something more but figure that's all he's good for.

For a moment you stand out on the sidewalk and look down the streets, busy with people familiar with this neighborhood.

"Nice purse," some grinning fool says as he passes by in a group.

You walk down the street a block and look, then another block, then you come back, go back into the lounge, and search again. You ask the bartender, the second bartender, nothing. Your mouth is dry and you feel sweat on your forehead. The music seems louder and the lights dimmer.

On the edge of a red couch, you open the purse. Menthol cigarettes, a tiny lighter, some makeup, a tiny wallet. You open the wallet and look for her license.

In the photo Jasmine stares at the camera without a smile. Hair a little shorter, a little darker.

Name: Jana Shreve.

Is Jana short for Jasmine? Or is Jasmine compensating for Jana? Or was it simply a bold-faced lie?

Jasmine's voice rings in your head.

Does it really matter?

You read the address. The street name doesn't mean anything, so in a shouting voice, you ask a nearby woman about the location. She tells you it's in Soho, just a few minutes away.

A sane man would leave the purse with the bartender and call it a night.

The plane leaves at nine in the morning, and you haven't gotten a lot of sleep lately.

You think of the threatening boyfriend and the two goons that took off with Jasmine. Or Jana.

Maybe she invites trouble. Maybe she's the sort that lives in a world full of this.

It's not your business so let it go.

But you can't.

You hold that license and look at the face and feel something. You don't know what. Desire? Lust? Affection? Fondness?

Curiosity?

Fear?

It's something.

Above everything, it's concern.

You're worried.

And again, maybe you're swimming in a sea of Long Island Iced Teas. But you're going to check. Just to be certain.

Just to be safe.

You go outside to get a cab and see if she might still live at the address on the license.

Maybe you'll find her there, safe and sound.

12:21 A.M.

SOMETHING SHARP JAMS INTO YOUR BACK and before you can turn around a voice says, "Get in the car."

For a moment you don't see it but then, down the street half a block, a black town car is waiting. Orange brake lights glow. You jerk your head, and the metal object presses hard against your spine.

"Walk."

This has got to be a joke. The best candid camera moment ever.

The voice is definitely not New York and definitely not friendly. You start toward the car, one hand still holding Jasmine's purse. Your head tries to get a good look at the source of the voice and now the gun barrel digs its way into your ear.

"Keep your eyes ahead and keep moving."

You reach the car and stop for a second. The voice tells you to get in.

"This isn't for show," he says.

You open the door and slide onto leather. A guy in a suit follows, his revolver still pointed at you.

"What—"

But before you can say anything, the door is closed and locked.

"Where is she?" the guy asks.

"Who?"

He grabs the purse from your hand. Now probably isn't the time to play stupid. The car accelerates down the street and the motion makes you feel a little queasy.

He's a young, twenty-something Asian without any sort of accent. He wears no expression on a cold and humorless face. The gun is aimed up at you. If he fired it now the bullet would come up underneath your chin and through your head.

Nice image, Mike.

"Who'd she leave with?"

"You probably know better than I do."

The guy has spiked hair that looks perfectly sculpted. He looks like he spends time in a tanning salon and a gym. His breath smells like peppermint.

"I'm asking you who she left with," he says, still in a flat, controlled voice.

"I have no idea. Two guys."

"What did she tell you?"

"She knew them. Or at least one of them. Some guy named Clark. Said she was going to go outside and talk for a few minutes."

"When was that?"

"What's this all about?" you ask.

"When did she leave?"

"I don't know. Half hour ago."

For having a gun in your face, you're doing pretty well at not freaking out. You look at the revolver and note how small it seems.

Is it real?

The car turns right and continues racing down the street. The driver has big, bushy hair. He acts like he's driven people held at gunpoint before.

"What do you want from me?" you ask.

The Asian guy looks at you with expressionless eyes. "You ever hear the sound of a head hitting pavement? Sounds like a watermelon splitting open. At this speed, you don't want me to throw you out of the car. Just answer my questions and maybe you'll get out of this alive."

Something in his tone makes you think he's not only serious, but he doesn't really care whether you live or die.

"How do you know J?"

"I just met her tonight," you admit.

The guy puts the gun in his lap and rummages through

the purse. He doesn't find anything he wants. You wonder about her license and remember you slipped it into your pants pocket.

"You chose a bad night to be picking up girls, mister."

"Nobody picked up anybody."

He laughs. "Yeah, uh-huh. What's your story?"

"I'm here on business."

"Hey, Carl," the Asian guy calls out to the driver. "He's here on business."

"Uh-huh," the driver says with a laugh.

"What kind of business?"

"Nothing that gets guns pointed at you."

"J likes to get herself in trouble. She's made an art out of it."

"Do I look like trouble?"

He laughs. His eyes are calculating and cold.

"You look like a moron who's had a little too much to drink."

"Then can you let me out?"

"Oh, we'll let you out. The question is, what sort of condition will you be in when we let you out."

"What's that mean?"

"Hey, Carl, want to tell him what that means?"

The driver keeps his eyes on the road but nods. "You ever hear about bodies showing up in the Hudson Bay? It's because they're really stupid."

The driver has a thick accent, as though he's from the Bronx. Or from Jersey.

"Now, they're not all stupid," the guy with the gun says. "Sometimes they know more than they're saying."

"What do you want to know? I don't even know her real name. She said it was Jasmine, but later I found out it was Jana."

The buildings are flying by, and you're continuing to feel slightly nauseated, not to mention freaked out.

"Any reason you were going through her purse?" the guy next to you asks.

"Because she disappeared."

"And you let her just disappear, huh?"

"I didn't *let* her do anything," you say. "The guys were— they were a lot like you."

"Don't insult us," the Asian says. "You know, if J gets in trouble, or if she disappears, then we're all in trouble. You know that?"

"What do you want me to do about it?"

"You might want to take better care of the women you try to pick up."

"Nobody was trying to pick anybody up."

"Oh, J definitely had something in mind for you. Carl, does J *ever* do anything with another man without wanting something in return?"

"Nope," the thick accent says.

"So, Mr. Innocent here. What happened?"

"Two guys came. One big and the other slick looking. They sat down and acted like they knew her. She went outside with them."

"And left her purse?"

"That's right."

He waits and watches you. There's nothing to hide.

"And at Atmosphere?"

How do you know about that?

"The guy was trying to hurt her," you say.

He nods.

"And you? You're just in the mix for no good reason, right?"

"Exactly."

He picks up the gun and puts the barrel against your forehead. You feel the metal jam into your skin, pressing hard against your skull.

"Does this get your heart racing?" he asks.

You can barely breathe. You try to breathe and still act and talk the same. "Yes, it does."

He laughs.

"I don't know if you're getting the point."

"I get it, please, I don't want—this is none of my business."

The guy presses his tongue against his lower teeth. He looks out the window and thinks for a minute.

"Sometimes J gets guys thinking. Thinking *too* much. Know what I mean?"

You nod but you don't have a clue what he's talking about.

"A guy like you. He might be thinking a little too much, you know? And that's a bad thing."

"I'm done thinking," you say.

And I was done thinking hours ago.

He strokes the edge of your face with the revolver. "I just don't get it. Why? Why does this always happens with J? Why? Tell me."

I don't know what you're talking about.

The man curses and looks outside at the passing streets. He laughs, then glances ahead at the driver.

"Carl, what do you think of this guy?"

"I say pop 'im in the head like they did in *Goodfellas.*"

"Good idea," the man beside you says with a grin. "You see that movie?"

You nod. You're starting to believe this guy is serious and you're thinking about grabbing the gun from his hands.

It might not be impossible. He's holding it loosely, too casually.

But another thought stops you.

What about Lisa and the kids?

What are you doing, Michael?

Don't do anything stupid don't try anything just calm down and stay relaxed and try to get out of this car alive.

"Bodies get stowed away in trunks. Happens all the time. Right, Carl?"

The driver laughs and nods.

"Now here's something. I could give you a little reminder of tonight. A shot in your thigh. Nothing too harmful. If you're lucky you won't bleed to death. Sometimes that happens, you know. But something that will make you remember this night."

"I'll remember," you say, the panic rising from deep inside you.

"He says he'll remember. What do you think of that, Carl?"

"They don't always," the driver says.

"Now Carl here, he prefers to simply beat the snot out of people. He likes getting his hands messy. Sorta like a mechanic doing an oil change who has oil dripping from his knuckles. The way he makes you remember—well, the mirror will do that for you."

Carl doesn't say anything and you know they're not joking.

"Where are you from?" the Asian asks.

You breathe in deeply and can't keep your body from shaking.

"Chicago."

"Chicago. Chi-caugh-go. Da Bears. Huh? Da Bulls."

You nod and keep looking at the gun.

Grab it. Just grab it and shove it in his face.

"You seem like a good guy. Right, Carl?"

"Seems pretty stupid to me," the driver says.

"But hey—if J picked you up, she must've done it for a reason. Maybe she was feeling charitable. Right?"

You nod.

The guy's face tightens, and his eyes sharpen as he studies you critically.

"I don't know why in God's name J decided to pick you up, but she did. And I'll just tell you something. You think you're scared right now? You don't want to mess with J. That woman is seriously demented. And I mean seriously."

He looks ahead at the driver and then seems to regain his focus.

"Do you understand that the best thing that can happen to you is for you to just disappear? And there's only one way I can *make* you disappear. Got that?"

You nod.

"So, now, let's say we let you go. You're going to leave J alone, right? I mean, she has enough distractions in her life without someone else bothering her. Right?"

Again you nod in agreement.

"You a resourceful man?"

"Sure," you say.

Just let me out of this car.

"Carl, this a good place?"

The driver nods. "Sure is. The next five or six blocks take the prize."

"Well, let's see just how resourceful you are."

The car slows down and you look around. You see a wall of graffiti where the car stops.

"Get out," the guy says.

A torn-down building to your right tells you it might be hard getting a cab.

"Here?" you ask, suddenly afraid of opening the door.

"You *so* want to get out of this car and away from me. You don't want to see me again. Got that? Not me, not J, not anybody else. Not tonight. Understand?"

He's holding the gun in your face again. You nod and open the car door. The night is cool and your legs feel stiff.

The car rushes away and you're left in a silent, dimly lit block somewhere in New York.

Somewhere in a very bad part of New York.

You're not in Soho anymore.

12:45 A.M.

YOU WOULD BE A LOT MORE SCARED if you weren't so drunk.

Maybe drunk is not the right word. You're above the legal limit, sure, but you can also walk in a straight line. At least when nobody is looking.

The reality is not only that you're in a run-down and desolate part of the city but that you're out past midnight with a gorgeous blonde grinning at you and holding your hand and guys with spiked hair and uncaring eyes pointing guns at you. This isn't your life.

There's no sidewalk on this street. A big two-story building next to you looks black and deathly empty. The closest streetlight is a block away. There's no sign of any cars or any life. Across from you stands the remains of a building that looks half gone.

You start to walk down the street, half hoping to see a car coming, half hoping the street stays this deserted.

Sometimes when you take out Jack the Lhasa Apso one last time to do his nightly duty, you can look up at the stars from your modest-sized backyard in the suburb of Deerfield. It's an expensive house and lot, and it's small moments like this that you pay for. But now, walking on this side street, you look up and see only grayish black. No stars, nothing.

You check your phone again and see that you missed a call. A symbol says that you have voice mail. You check it and hear Lisa's voice.

"Hey—where are you? You're not going to believe what happened before bedtime. Jack wallowed in crap again, and I had to clean him up. I love how he only does this when you're out of town. I swear. Call me if you can. Sorry to hear about the dinner. Peyton played with his mac and cheese at my parents'. Olivia didn't eat anything. Typical dinner. Love you."

Lisa's voice sounds so out of place here and now. You miss her. You miss the normalcy of seeing her. You miss resting by her right now.

Because you're scared.

You tell yourself you're not scared, but you are. It's just coming over you right now, the wave of fear that should have covered you in the car.

You've got a wife and two children.

You know that and you always know that. You leave the

house and go to bed thinking that. It's branded on your heart and soul. But sometimes—sometimes—you want to forget. You want to simply have a drink and a good time and not worry so much. You don't want so much weighing you down.

Too late.

You wonder what you were thinking. But you know. You know what you were thinking the moment you dialed those numbers. There was a slight hope, a slight tease. You thought maybe, perhaps, possibly

just maybe

and wanted to see where the night took you.

Atmosphere.

345.

That's where it took you.

And now here, wherever here is.

Good job, Mike.

You delete Lisa's voice mail and notice there's another.

You listen to the second voice mail and stop when Jasmine's erratic voice comes on the line.

"My God, Mike, I can't—you gotta help me. I don't know—I'm sorry—I don't know who else to—I'm at Exit, this club—please come—"

And then nothing.

You hear muffled noise in the background—a street or a public place or something like that.

The phone number is unlisted. You can't redial.

You remember that her license is still in your pocket.

I can at least go and see if she's back home by now.

You just had a gun pointed at you, waved in your face, brushed up against your cheek.

Those guys weren't kidding.

They dropped you off in the middle of nowhere. You should be glad you're alive.

Enough's enough, Mike.

But you're not tired and you're worried about Jasmine. She might be a flirt and frivolous and flippant but she's still a young woman and you don't want to see her hurt.

Jasmine's going to be fine. She'll be okay. You don't need to protect her.

But maybe she wanted and needed protection. Maybe she's reaching out for someone to save her.

And maybe, just maybe, that someone is you.

1:05 A.M.

YOUR HEAD HURTS. BURNS. STINGS.

The adrenaline is slowing down but you still hurt.

You look around and keep walking.

Walk. Step. Step.

You have no idea where you are and you're a little afraid.

A little?

Maybe a lot.

You check your phone. Who can you call? The cops?

Call them.

To say what? To do what?

Are you really in trouble? Does being in a bad part of the city necessarily mean—

"Hey."

You turn to see a car slowing down. You stop looking when you see the figures in the car.

"Looks like you're lost," the voice says, laughing.

You keep walking.

"Slow down there now."

You walk faster.

"We ain't gonna do anything."

But there are three of them and you are sticking out.

Sticking way out.

"Buddy, come on over here."

And you look and see the grin and the glistening, hazy eyes and think it might be best for you to start hauling tail out of here.

You begin to sprint down the sidewalk. The street feels hard beneath your shoes and you suck in air but you feel like you could run five miles this way.

The engine behind you revs up but you don't bother looking. You keep running down the sidewalk until you come to a narrow alley.

It's too small for a car to go down.

You don't bother looking to see where it heads. You go down it, the darkness of the two buildings on each side making it impossible to see all the way down.

You hear the squeal of tires stopping. The sound of car doors opening.

"Come on, man!" someone shouts at you. "Come on back here!"

But you keep running. You're not going to look back and you're not going to stop.

You feel air and suck in air and feel the alley walls closing in and hear the echoes of your footsteps.

You can sense them coming after you.

A wall stops you dead in your tracks. It's a wood fence, about six feet tall.

You look back and see three figures walking toward you.

A curse escapes out of your mouth. You put one hand on the top of the fence and then try to scale the wall.

Nothing. You fall back.

They're still coming.

You try again. This time, you manage to scale the wall and hoist your body high enough to drape one leg over the wall.

You try to pull the rest over. One second passes. Nothing. Another.

You're about to fall off.

Come on Mike do it pull yourself up.

"Where you think you're going?" a voice asks.

You finally manage to get another leg over. You pull and get the rest of your body over the fence. It feels unsturdy as you get behind it and feel your feet fall to the concrete street.

You don't bother looking behind. You keep running down the rest of the alley, opening up to another street.

Call someone.

You look right and left. Neither looks particularly appealing. Empty, dark streets. Deserted, blackened shells of buildings.

Right or left. Pick your poison.

You head right and start running. You run. And keep running. Until your chest feels like it's going to explode. And your legs have to stop. You suck in air. And you try to listen to see if you can hear anything. For the moment, it's nothing but silence.

1:24 A.M.

BEFORE A VOICE CAN WARN YOU to go the other way, you hear the sound of the engine racing down the street, then slowing and pulling up close to you. You can't help but feel your breath catch as you see the dark face smoking a cigarette behind the jacked-up Cadillac SUV.

"You lost there?" a low voice asks above the raucous beat of the dance music.

"I'm fine, thanks," you say, not even looking at the driver, walking on.

"I don't think you're fine, man."

You keep walking.

"You know where you are?"

You look at him and see his eyes below thick dreadlocks. There is a humor in them, laced with friendliness.

"Actually, I don't."

"Your car broke down?"

"It's been a long night."

He laughs. "Gonna be a lot longer if you don't get in the car."

His voice and his attitude seem friendly enough. You survived the gun in your face, you can tackle this.

You get into the car. The driver is a big African-American with funky, bright clothes and a mass of dreads. The interior smells like cologne and is remarkably clean. The leather feels good.

"So what's your story?" he asks as he accelerates down the empty street.

Glowing red numbers on the dash read 1:24 a.m. The bass almost massages you as the driver heads down streets as if he knows where he's going.

"You won't believe it."

"You're not from around here, huh?"

"Chicago," you say.

"You live in New York long enough, you'll get to see everything. But a white guy wandering around this part of the Bronx at one in the morning—now that's a first for me."

"This is the Bronx?"

He laughs, a deep guttural laugh that makes you do the same. "Yeah, a very nasty section. Don't even ask what I'm doing driving down here. But you—you gotta have a story."

"It started with meeting a chick."

The driver curses in amusement. "Stop there. No need to say anything else."

"Half an hour ago someone had a gun in my face."

He curses again, now in astonishment. "What for?"

"Info on the woman."

"And what's her story?"

You shrug. "Just met her today."

He looks at you with eyes that look tired and glassy. "Just met her today, huh?"

You nod.

"How long you been married?"

For a minute you think he noticed your wedding ring, but you remember you left it back at the hotel.

"How'd you—"

"Man, you've got married written all over you. That 'just met her today' comment. Major guilt, man."

"Twelve years."

"What's her name?"

"Lisa."

He nods. "Kids?"

"Two."

"So a call in the middle of the night to Lisa saying her hubby was found in the south Bronx with a couple rounds in his head wouldn't be so good, right?"

"I just wanted to get out of that car."

"Like being married?"

The question is simple and straightforward.

"Where are you going?"

"Heading toward Midtown," the driver says.

You find the license and ask to turn on the light.

"What's that?"

"The woman I met."

He takes the license from you and curses. "She looks like this?"

You nod.

"And you let her get away?"

"Didn't have much of a choice. Any chance you're heading toward there?"

"That's the Village."

"That's where I need to go."

The guy nods. "You didn't answer my question."

"Yeah, marriage is good."

You say this without thinking. The guy's laugh surprises you.

"What?"

"Good, huh?"

You're tired and your buzz is wearing off and you should be heading back to the hotel but you can't.

"It's hard work too," you say.

"So you gotta keep things exciting, huh?"

"Not *this* exciting."

"Just got engaged a month ago."

"Congrats."

"I'm Tupac," the driver says.

"Michael."

You look at him and he's laughing. "Man, I'm just teasin'. My name's Walt."

Any other time, you'd come up with a witty retort. But you're too tired and too out of it to think of anything.

"So twelve years and two kids—what's that have to do with that license?"

"Nothing."

"Nothing, huh?"

"Yeah, I can't explain it."

Walt laughs and stops the SUV at the red light. He looks over at you. "You don't have to explain it. She's hot. Enough said."

You want to say *She came up to me.* You want to say *She invited me out.* But those are lame excuses. Lisa would say so and so what and you're so in trouble.

I didn't do anything.

"So what now?" Walt asks.

"What?"

"You seeing her again?"

"Hoping to. She left me a voice mail—she might be in a little trouble."

"Serious?"

You nod.

The song changes and the laughter starts and Walt turns up the stereo as the funky beat goes in unison to the high-pitched voice singing "Feel Good."

What would it feel like to be twenty-one again? To be engaged again? To be free again? To not have to think of the responsibilities and the ring on your finger and those snapshots in your head? You wouldn't give up anything, but sometimes on occasions you wish you could be single and twenty-something again just for the night.

But you're not, Mike.

You're thirty-seven and you're an adult. You're not hip and you're not young and you can't do anything you want.

There are consequences to actions.

The Cadillac drives smoothly and the music soothes you. The deserted and empty outside has been replaced by traffic and people and life and energy. It's amazing how quickly conditions can change in a matter of miles.

You look over at Walt, and his shoulders move as if he's ready to dance. His lips mime the words and he seems to forget you're here.

Maybe it's time to go back to the hotel.

But you remember Jasmine's last voice mail. You have to do something. At least check out her place, see if she's there. If she's not, you can call the cops and then leave the rest to them. Then get some rest and head home later this morning.

"Got any advice?" the driver asks you.

"On what?"

"The whole marriage thing. I mean, twelve years. You must be doing something right."

All that comes to your mind are a dozen things you've done wrong.

"Once the whole honeymoon period ends—and believe me, it always does—you have to be open and honest. If you go too long not being honest, that spells disaster."

"My fiancée—she's brutally honest. I don't think she'll ever have a problem with that whole area."

Yeah, but it takes two to be completely honest.

"Just be patient. And remember—it's hard work."

"And don't go chasing broads in the middle of the night," Walt says.

You laugh. "Yeah."

"But you're going to try to find her, aren't you?"

"I'm just afraid—I don't know. I'm afraid she might be in a lot of trouble."

"What exactly are you gonna do?"

"Good question."

I don't have a clue. But at least I'll know. At least I'll be able to see if she's okay.

As the driver listens and sings along to the music, you feel a new sensation on this night. The sense of danger and adventure, something your life has sorely lacked. Where is that sense of adventure and thrill seeking that you used to long for as a boy but suddenly forgot about once adulthood came into play?

Having children is supposed to help with your sense of adventure. Right? It's supposed to keep you young at heart.

For once, your heart is racing and you feel alive and you feel that you're finally on an exciting journey.

What if that journey ends with a bullet in your head, Mike?

There are responsibilities that you have to think about.

What if something happens to Jasmine?

The SUV stops in the middle of a side street.

"It's gotta be one of these buildings around here," Walt says.

You shake his hand. "Hope this wasn't too far out of your way."

"Nah, it's cool."

"Thanks for being my guardian angel tonight."

"Can angels be black?" he asks with a laugh.

He finds something in the center near the dash and hands it to you.

"That's my card. Not that you're likely to be needing a DJ anytime soon. But it's got my cell number on it. Anybody puts a gun in your face again, or you end up in the south Bronx, give me a call, all right?"

"Appreciate it."

He nods and you exit the car. The music grows louder and he drives off.

You replace his card with the license from your pocket. You see the address and walk down the street, trying to find it, trying to find something, trying to make sure that Jasmine is okay.

1:40 A.M.

You haven't told anyone about the counseling that Lisa and you have been going through the past year.

Lisa initiated it. You went willingly, thinking it was unnecessary, just a formality. Twelve years of marriage and you need counseling? Of course you don't. It's just this time of your life.

Lately, that's been the phrase you've been using. The Season Of Life You're In.

How come each season seems to be getting colder, darker, busier? When will spring ever come again? When things felt young and fresh and alive.

When things got really dark, you guys decided to keep at it. And that was when Lisa got pregnant. Olivia wasn't the result of trying another way out—both of you wanted a child. And for several years, Olivia and then Peyton managed to cover some of the dysfunctions. But they started to creep back in, more so recently than ever.

The counseling sessions have been fine. But sometimes you leave not telling the whole truth. You don't talk about this empty feeling you have. You don't tell them that lately you've been hearing a whole lot of silence from God.

It's your relationship with Lisa you're in counseling for, not your relationship with God.

You haven't said much to your church friends. In fact, you haven't seen much of them. The longstanding monthly small group you're in has been meeting less and less often. You use trips and work and the children as excuses. But you know the real reason. You don't want to admit failure. You don't want to tell them you've been angry at God for some time. People don't like hearing that sort of honest talk. So you've been staying away. And going through the motions whenever those friends are around.

It's just a season.

Just a season you're in.

But every day dims away and every morning brightens again and there you are, in the same season. With the same cloudy forecast.

Sometimes you want to run.

Running away from the car back there in the run-down neighborhood of the Bronx—sure, it was terrifying. But a part of you has needed something to jolt you back to reality. To resuscitate you. To bring you back up to the surface.

The counselor would have a heyday with a listing of tonight's exploits.

Time to take it up a level, Michael. Time to increase the dosage. Time to put on the headgear and inject shock treatment.

But you don't need shock treatment because this night is enough of a shock.

And the scary thing is that it's not over. It's far from over.

I need help but I can't ask for help because I'm angry at the only person who can give it to me.

1:46 A.M.

THE GUY BEHIND THE DESK BUZZES you in through the door to the lobby of the high-rise. He's got a big neck and his eyes look tired.

"Yeah?" he asks.

"I need to see Jas—Jana Shreve."

"I can call up to her place."

"Okay, yeah, that'd be great."

He spends a minute on the phone and watches you suspiciously. The gel on his hair glows off the warm orange lights of the narrow hallway.

"She's not there."

"Any chance I can leave a message?"

"With me."

"I have her license."

"Yeah? How'd you get that?"

"She left her purse at a bar."

The doorman looks at you again. "You know J?"

"Yes. Sort of."

"Right. So where's her purse?"

"Long story."

"Must've been a busy night."

"Why's that?" you ask.

"Guy came by about an hour ago or so asking for J. A little more frantic than you."

"What'd he look like?"

"He had a busted nose, I know that. Short guy."

"I think he's part of the problem."

"What problem is that?"

"Any way you know how to get ahold of her?"

He shakes his head and laughs. "You got any idea who she is?"

"No."

"One of the richest families in New York. She could be Paris Hilton if she wanted to. Her parents pay for this." He gestured toward the lobby. "And for everything else she has."

"Think anybody might want to hurt her?"

The guy laughs and lets out a curse. "Man, a whole lot of people might want to hurt her. Or do something to her. You've seen her. A girl that hot has to be careful."

He pauses, then continues.

"Thing is, J's not careful. That girl is trouble."

I realize that.

"Any idea where she might be?"

"You think she's in trouble?" he asks.

"Maybe."

"Some might say to call her parents, but not me. They're a little—I don't know—crazy? A little crazy protective."

"Ever heard of a place called Exit?"

"Probably a club. J's into those."

You think for a moment and then decide to leave your name and number with the man. He takes it without comment or reaction.

For some reason you hold on to Jasmine's license.

Back on the street, you think for a moment. Maybe it's time to head back to the hotel. Sleep is not what you need. You need a closed door and a safe room.

A hand grabs your arm, and you swing around, ready to hit somebody.

It's Amanda. Jasmine's friend. She looks frantic, out of breath, and astounded.

"What are you doing here?"

"Your friend disappeared."

"I know. Have you—did you just come from her apartment?"

"They wouldn't let me in."

"Yeah, I know. Come on."

She leads you back into the apartment building.

"Hey, Danny."

The security guard is suddenly a little more animated, seeing her.

"You're back."

You nod and follow Amanda into the open elevator.

"You live here too?" you ask her.

"I come here enough. I have a key."

"Is Jasmine here?"

Amanda glances at you for a second.

"Or J? Whatever her name is."

"I don't think so. I'm a little worried."

"Yeah, me too."

"Where'd she go? I got a voice mail from her."

"We went to a place. I forget the name. It's got numbers—"

"345."

"That's it," you say as the numbers ding off in the small elevator. "A couple guys sat down next to us. Scary-looking guys. She acted like she knew them."

"J knows everybody."

"She disappeared. Next thing I knew, someone was holding a gun in my face and dropping me off in some dead-end neighborhood."

Amanda shakes her head and laughs. "You're having a great night, huh?"

"I'm just a little worried for her."

"I'm always worried for J. That girl gives me ulcers."

The door opens to a small hallway with only four doors. Amanda searches through her purse and finds the key.

"I think I stay here more than she does."

"How long have you guys been friends?"

Amanda inserts the key. "Long enough. We're quasi-sisters. More or less."

The door swings open, and Amanda waits for you to go in.

"Go ahead. It's okay."

You nod but you don't feel okay. You don't know what's waiting behind that open doorway, inside this apartment, inside this continually evolving world.

You take a step, then another. Amanda follows you and closes the door.

She turns on a switch and several canned lights go on, illuminating the spacious, high-ceiling loft.

"Nice little place, huh?"

Everything is modern and tidy. A two-piece sofa looks like it's never been sat on. Black is the main color, with vibrant patches of orange or red in various places. You notice the plasma television screen on the wall, the Bose speakers in all four corners of the living room, the wet bar next to a mantel full of picture frames. There is a massive painting that looks just like Jasmine.

Amanda anticipates your question. "Some big painter in New York did that for her. For free."

She walks over to the kitchen and checks the phone for messages. "Want something to drink?"

You're thinking no, you don't really want anything, but you say yes, sure. Yes, sure. That's what you've been saying all night. Yes, sure.

"We've got a *lot* of vodka. Name it and we got it. J collects it. She likes the colorful bottles."

"Anything."

"Screwdriver? Or wait, let me see."

She opens the stainless steel refrigerator that is stocked full of everything. You see two full packages of bagels, beer, wine, Gatorade, bottled Evian, everything in its nice, neat order.

"I'll take a Becks," you say, trying to make it easier.

"Oh, sure? We've got everything."

She hands you the beer as you continue to examine this unlived-in loft.

"Clean, huh?"

"Does she even live here?"

"You can't put J in a box."

Amanda fixes herself what looks like a martini. She takes a bottle out of the freezer to make it.

"Where do you think she is?"

"No calls," Amanda says. "She'll call soon."

"She called me."

The redhead takes a sip from her glass and doesn't look

worried. "J is a drama queen. They need to do a reality TV show with her."

You see assorted pictures of Jasmine around her kitchen. All placed for show, not tossed up on the fridge with magnets. Jasmine in a tiny bikini on the shores of some tropical paradise. Jasmine in Paris. At a bar with friends. With a good-looking older couple, probably her parents. With her arm around . . . Brad Pitt?

"Ever wonder why some people are so blessed?" Amanda says, glancing at the same photos you're staring at. "Why some people get it all and don't even have to ask?"

"Yeah, I think about it."

The merger crosses your mind again, the deal that went south, the deal that brought you here, the deal you couldn't close.

"Why is it that women like Jana can get men to do almost anything?"

Her tone is different suddenly. You look at her and watch her drain her martini the way a college student might pound a beer.

"Tell me something," Amanda says, walking up close to the counter you lean against. "Would you be looking all over the city for me?"

There is a glint in her eye, something you can't necessarily place, something that makes you feel a bit nervous. "Sure I would," you say, not very convincingly.

Amanda picks up a picture, the one with Jasmine on a beach in her little white bikini.

"You either have it or you don't, you know? I am a size smaller than J and it doesn't matter. I can spend four hours a day on myself and never even be in the same vicinity. Why does a girl that gorgeous have to have everything too? Why is that?"

You take a sip of your beer and walk away from the kitchen, toward the living room. Canned lights illuminate the area.

"What is this?" you ask, trying to change the subject.

Amanda fixes herself another martini and tells you about the piece of art sitting on the end table. It looks like someone found it in a garbage heap. Next to it rest all the latest fashion magazines: *Cosmopolitan, Vogue, Elle.* The dates reveal them to be brand-new.

"She gets those replaced every month. Sometimes when she's bored—and *if* she's ever here—she'll read them. But they get replaced like clockwork. Like the milk in the fridge that goes untouched. I don't even know why she has them put milk in the fridge because she never drinks it. But you have to have milk in the fridge, right? I mean, of course you do. Not to have it would be just that. Not having something. And Jana always has everything."

An iPod rests in a Bose docking station on another table. Next to it is a framed photo of a Chihuahua.

"So, Steve?"

"It's Mike."

"Yeah, Mike. Come over here."

Amanda is on her second martini and sits on the couch, one long leg crossed over the other. She pats the seat next to her.

"Look—I just want to—I'd like to know where your friend disappeared to."

"Did you guys get a chance to have any fun?"

The look on Amanda's face is mischievous and wild, almost scary.

"Come on," she says after your silence. "You look like you saw a ghost. Look—I've got a little something that can make you feel a lot better."

"I'm fine, really."

She stands and comes by you. The glass on the coffee table is empty. She twirls a finger under one of the buttons of your shirt and pulls it toward herself.

"I won't bite," she says with a laugh.

Didn't Jasmine say that too?

Though she looked attractive at first, this close, you see that Amanda wears a lot of makeup. Her eyes look cold and her lips fake. She's pale and almost anorexic, and nothing about her appeals to you. She tells you to follow her and walks toward a hallway and a dark room.

She turns on the lights and turns around, looking at you standing still in the same place you were.

"Come on. I just want to show you Jana's room. And what she keeps in there."

Really it's okay it's fine I'm fine this is fine everything is going to be fine everything's gonna be just fine.

"Look, I'm really okay."

"Come on. I swear, I won't force you to do anything. It won't hurt."

What is she talking about? What won't hurt? Amanda won't hurt you? Is this all some game?

You walk toward the bedroom and enter it, another large room with high ceilings and simple, straightforward styling. The large bed sits in the middle of the room, all black. Amanda sits on the edge of it and takes off one of her high heels.

"These things have been killing me all day."

"Look, I think I should go," you say.

Amanda laughs and curses at the same time. "God, I want a cigarette. Do you smoke? One thing we never do in here is smoke. You can't smoke anywhere in this ungodly city."

There is a room off to the side of this uncluttered bedroom. You want to get away from Amanda and this place.

"Can I—I'm going to use the bathroom."

"Right in there," she says, taking her other shoe off.

You wonder if she's going to keep going. Maybe you should bolt out of here. This is crazy. This is crazy and what would anybody you know think of this right now.

You search the wall for a light and turn it on. It's a large bathroom with two sinks and a separate room with a walk-in closet. You walk by the closet heading to the toilet and

what the

lift up the toilet lid and then realize what you just saw.

A face, in the darkness, staring out at you.

Before you can turn around, before you can suck in a breath, before you can put your arms out or above you or in front of you, something hits you on the back of your head.

And the only thing your mind sees as you go black is the face of Riley, the curly short hair, his lips laughing, grinning, cackling. But then the face turns into Jasmine. Then you're out.

SOMETIME BETWEEN
1:57 - 2:23 A.M.

THE DARKNESS LANDS ON THE LIGHT of a candle, a small lit flame burning in the middle of the table, illuminating her slender hands and the wedding band you gave her years earlier. You look up to see the flickering shadows against her shirt, her neck, her chin, her little button nose, her brown eyes, her brown hair.

"I'm just tired of everything," you say.

You've had a few drinks tonight and maybe that's allowing you to talk. You're not saying anything you haven't felt for a while. It's just that you've been so busy and Lisa has been so busy and now that you both have come up for air and can actually sit across from one another without an obligation or a cell phone going off or something to do, you feel the waves of reality rushing over you.

"Tired of what?"

She's not shocked and shouldn't be shocked.

But what are you saying. Really?

"Tired of living next to you but not really being with you."

"What does that mean?"

You have another sip of the wine. Wine does wonders on you. A few glasses and you feel the weight of the world slip away. This is vacation and you're allowed to have that feeling. But you're not feeling good and you haven't felt good for some time.

"It means—I don't know what it means. Why do I have to be the one to bring this up?"

"I asked you what was wrong," Lisa says.

"I don't know exactly what's wrong."

"I thought—getting away—spending some time on the beach and away from it all—I thought that would be good."

"Maybe . . ." But you can't finish your thought.

"What?"

"Nothing."

"What?"

Lisa knows what you were about to say and you know that she knows. She just wants you to say it. To be a man and say it and get it on the table.

Say it. Go ahead, Mike, and say it. Just say the truth. Say what you're thinking.

"Maybe we need to get away from each other."

There. I said it.

She looks at you, the face of a woman you used to love, that you don't know if you love now, a face that you trusted and that once trusted you. Hurt and confusion and anger pour down over that sweet face.

"I'm just—"

"What does that mean?" she asks.

Except she's not asking. She's demanding to know.

"I don't know."

But a part of you knows what you mean. Part of you simply doesn't want to acknowledge it.

You're not one of those couples and never could be one of those couples and always knew you were different from one of those many couples that tried to make it work but couldn't and finally gave up.

I'm not giving up.

But telling yourself is one thing. You know your heart and your soul and your mind and they all feel this way.

They all gave up some time ago. You can't remember when, but they gave in.

And now . . . you look into eyes that no longer mesmerize you. They only hurt you.

Where did it all go wrong?

And then this picture, this faint memory, goes out, like the flame of a candle blown out too quickly.

2:24 A.M.

YOU OPEN YOUR MOUTH and your tongue licks your lips and then what you discover to be the tile floor of Jasmine's bathroom. Your hand goes instantly for the back of your head, where you feel a knot the size of a golf ball. For a moment you just lie there, unable to move, unable to see. The light is still on and you eventually manage to move your body and your head and everything up.

A wave of nausea pulses through you. You fight it and gain control and open your eyes.

Nothing. You look in toward the bedroom and see no one. You listen but don't hear anything.

Your hand continues to rub down the knot. You look at your watch but have no idea how long you were out.

For a second you think of something and then reach for your wallet in your back pocket. It's still there.

You try to recall what happened. Amanda showing you the room, taking off her shoes on the edge of the bed. You going to the bathroom, then . . .

The image in your mind is of Riley. But you don't know this for sure. You can barely remember what the guy looks like. And the closet was pitch black.

You could see the outline of a figure in there. That was it.

In your mind you curse and you use your arms to help you get up. For a moment you stand against the bathroom counter, then the wave of nausea presses through you again.

You find that toilet you were looking for and throw up everything in your stomach. It's quick and for a moment you're resting your head against the bowl and feeling the tears in your eyes and the grit in your mouth.

Praying to the ceramic gods, as they said in college.

You get back to your feet and rinse your mouth and wash your face with cold water and then take a soft black towel and rub down your face and your forehead.

The man facing you in the mirror looks scared and tired and out of his mind.

What are you doing here, Michael? Tell me that. What are you thinking? Are you really out of your mind?

You walk out of the bathroom slowly, waiting to hear anything or see anything. But there is nothing.

Everything is in its place. Nobody is there. Not Amanda, no one.

You go into the living room and sit on the couch and decide to finish the remnants of your beer to get rid of the gross taste in your mouth.

I gotta go back to my hotel and leave this insanity behind.

There is a high-pitched ring and you jerk and cover your head before you realize it's the phone.

You look for it and find the cordless phone in the kitchen.

It rings four times and then clicks off. Two seconds later, it starts ringing again.

This time you pick it up. You don't say a word.

"Hello? Hello?"

You recognize Jana's voice.

"Jasmine," you say.

"Michael? Is that—how did you—what are you doing there?"

"Your friend let me in."

"Who?"

"Amanda."

"Is she there—what are you guys—"

"Are you okay?"

"No."

She sounds out of breath and panicked. Your head hurts too bad to pick up the pace.

"Where are you?"

"I'm still at Exit. I just got a call—Riley said he's coming to hurt me—did he—what happened?"

"Someone just knocked me unconscious."

There is a pause and you wonder what she's doing on the other end. There is faint music and crowd noise in the background.

"You have to leave. Just leave me alone and go away."

"Jasmine . . ."

"No—Michael, you have to stay out of this. I mean—I don't know what I was thinking. Listen to me, my name isn't even Jasmine."

"I know. It's Jana."

"Yes. And this—this was a bad night. Just hear me out—"

"No, you hear me out," you say, the adrenaline kicking in, the anger suddenly coursing all throughout. "If this Riley did this to me, then he might be coming to do something to you."

"It's not your concern."

"You made it my concern," you say.

"Michael—"

"Just stay there, okay? Stay around people, okay?"

"What are you going to do?"

That's a good question. What *are* you going to do?

"I'm going to come and get you."

"And then what?"

"I don't know. Let's figure that out, okay?"

"I just—Amanda just called me—"

"Don't trust Amanda," you say.

"What?"

"Just—just be careful, okay? I mean, I have no idea what's going on. I just—my head is killing me. I'll be there in a few minutes and then we can get out of there and go somewhere."

"I'm sorry, Michael," she says, almost starting to cry.

"It's okay. Really, it's okay. I'll be there in a few minutes. Just, just be careful and stay out in the open around people and avoid Riley."

You hang up the phone and then look around one more time.

You can turn around and go back.

You open the fridge and take out a Gatorade to drink and get rid of the foul taste in your mouth.

You have your second or third or fourth wind. You're heading to get Jasmine.

Nothing else to think about.

2:45 A.M.

THE NIGHT BURNS OUTSIDE as the cab passes through it. You feel a chill even though your window is only slightly cracked. The streets don't know you and you don't know them. A strange man in a strange land.

What am I doing here?

And you can't fully answer that question.

A beautiful face and a stunning body and golden hair and haunting eyes and you're lost. Just like that.

It wasn't that simple.

There's more to the story. A weakness deep down. Something you try to keep in check and in balance but that sometimes gets to you and sometimes overpowers you.

The world tempts you.

The world wants you.

And sometimes, sometimes, you dip your foot into it. Nobody has to know and nobody has to care.

God knows.

And you know this and sometimes you want him not to look and not to care. Sometimes you need to run far away from him so he might not see. A distant city with another name and the late hours of the night and how will he care? What can you do to make him notice?

He knows and he cares.

And so what? What are you going to do? Nothing. Right? Nothing at all.

A compromise here and a concession there. Being a man in today's world is a hard thing. Being a man of faith in today's world is downright impossible. Being pure and being faithful and being holy. How?

There is a way, Mike, there is only one way.

And you remain true. But sometimes in some places you occasionally let yourself go.

Jasmine.

It was just a name and a number. And you had to call and had to try and had to go down this road.

The cab turns a corner and heads down a street surrounded by industrial buildings. You wonder if you're in the right section of town.

You think of the conversation you had with Lisa awhile

ago about the Internet. About some of the links she found. About some of the pages she came across.

It's simple and easy and anonymous and you went there just like you called that number and for a while there was no consequence. But there was hurt and there was admission.

What if Jasmine or Jana or J had come right out with what you wanted? What you secretly hoped?

I want you Michael and I want you tonight and there are no consequences and no costs and no guilt and no strings. Free love and that's all.

But everything has a price and a string attached to it. If not down here then certainly up there.

I'm trying to get away from you God because I haven't heard a lot from you lately.

Being busy isn't an excuse and you know that.

The driver stops in front of one of those unmarked unnamed buildings and calls out the address.

"Want to stick around to make sure I got the right place?"

"Yeah, no problem."

You give him a twenty and tell him to keep the change. Surely this isn't the right place.

The gray-black walls seem to go for half a block. But out of nowhere you see a door with a man standing next to it. This has been a night full of guys guarding things. People and places. The guy isn't huge but he looks mean and just waits for you to say something.

"I'm here with J Shreve."

He looks at you as if you're not following the dress code. Maybe the name isn't good enough to get in. Maybe you need to say something else.

But he opens the steel door and lets out the pounding music and you enter yet another club and feel the heat and are lost in a dark hallway that has pulsing red lights at the end that glow and shadow a small sign on the wall that reads EXIT.

One more choice, Mike. One more chance. One more opportunity to exit this, all of this.

But you turn and walk into the massive club and know that the night is far from done and that you're not free and that you can't exit this that you're much too far in and that you have to play this out.

3:00 A.M.

WHEN YOU'RE A KID, you dream of rescuing the damsel in distress.

The prince always comes and rescues her.

In those stories, and those dreams, the princess always has long blonde hair. Does she have long legs too?

When you sit behind a desk and work on a computer all day dealing with figures and spreadsheets and financials, you have zero adventure and romance in your life.

Does that justify your being here at this time of night?

In some ways, it does. At least to yourself. You're not a bad guy and you're not doing a bad thing.

What happens if you find Jasmine? Then what?

The thrill of this, all of this, is part of what keeps you going. When was the last time you had passion in your life? Adventure? Romance?

Romance isn't a weekend getaway in Chicago.

Adventure isn't spending ten bucks at the movie theatre to see the latest action flick.

And passion isn't imagining what life would be like if you had this or did that or felt this or lived that.

Right now, you're in the middle of adventure and romance and passion.

You have no idea how this night is going to end. But you're doing a good thing, making sure Jasmine is okay.

You have good motivations.

They are fine motivations.

You need to find her and make sure she gets home safely.

And then . . .

And then, there will be choices to make.

You are a good man and you will do what's right.

The prince always does what's right.

Right?

3:06 A.M.

A FISHBOWL OF MOVING BODIES and bare arms and glowing fore-heads and glassy eyes surrounds you. Lights flicker and pulsate and each time you see a different image, a different contortion of figures. You're invisible and the others that surround you are oblivious. You can feel the bass and the beat in your soul as your breathe in the murky air created by smoke machines and sweat.

You feel your phone vibrate and you open it up.

It's Jasmine's phone number. By now it's as familiar as anyone else's in your phone.

You listen but can't begin to hear anything. You move toward one of the walls to try to hear better.

"Can you hear me?" you shout into the phone. "Where are you? Are you okay?"

Nothing. You close the phone and wander up an immense staircase, hoping to get away from the beats. The phone buzzes again.

"Yeah?"

You hear music and the phone cutting in and out. Jasmine's voice cracks and you can barely make out "trying to find" or something like that.

"Are you still here?" you shout as you head up the stairs.

All you get are jumbled noises, probably the same that you hear all around you.

She's somewhere in this huge club. There seem to be multiple levels.

You enter a room playing hip-hop with a small group on the dance floor and a larger group around a bar. It's dark and you can barely make out any faces. You try and look for Jasmine's outfit, for long legs that match her, for the blonde hair that's impossible to not notice.

Looking around, you wonder if you missed out on a whole other part of life. Is this a typical Friday night for all of these people? Who are they and where do they come from?

Twenty-somethings not looking for anything. Not worried about time and consequences and fears and responsibilities.

You stand at the edge of the dance floor looking like a spectator, a bystander. That's what you've done most of your life. Even in high school and college. Always watching. Looking on as others did it all. Watching people get drunk at parties. Watching your friends as they climbed in bed with some nameless girl for a harmless night.

But was it really harmless?

You've always believed that no, it's not harmless. But you've been curious. Why is it that you've obeyed the rules and walked the straight line and still have little to show for it?

You have a wife and two children waiting back home.

And a job in jeopardy and a career that's flatlining. A mother who's slowly losing her mind to Alzheimer's. And a faith that's dwindling.

You know your place in the world.

You used to. But not anymore. Not for some time.

In the shadowed corner, a couple makes out without a care for watchers. A trio tries to dance as one on the floor. A man sitting at the bar shakes his glass and wipes his eyes.

It's the dead of night and this is where the soulless dwell.

You have to find Jasmine and make sure she's okay and then get out of here.

A side room contains another bar with television monitors showing sports. You feel the vibration of your phone again.

"Where are you?" her voice shouts above the music.

"Some room in Exit. Are you okay?"

"I need to find you."

"I'm on the second level. In a—it's just a small bar with television screens and tables in it."

"Just—hold on."

"Is everything—?"

But the line is dead.

You go up to the bar and order a beer. Your throat is raw and your mouth dry and your head throbs.

You sit on a bar stool and wait. The beer tastes good and you finish it quickly and order another.

A figure comes down the stairway wearing tight dark jeans and a silk camisole top that looks more like a teddy than a shirt. You see the blonde hair bound to one side and then see Jasmine's eyes looking at yours.

When did she change?

You stand and before you can say something she gives you a hug. You're immersed in her sweet smell and you close your eyes and want to stay like this for a long time. Your mouth and your nose and face all inhale her blonde hair so soft and so silky.

"I'm so glad you're here."

"Did I miss something?" you ask as you look her over.

"Oh, God, I need a drink."

"We should leave."

"Everything's fine." She grins. "You're here now."

"Are you sure?"

"Yes. Just—just stay by me."

The look she gives you makes you feel confident, like you're her protector. For the moment, maybe you are.

The prince and the princess.

"What do you want?" you ask and get it for her as she sits on a bar stool. You can hear the thumping beat from music in the other room.

You bring her the martini and sit across from her.

"Are you okay?"

She nods and takes a sip from her glass. She lets out a sigh and then curses, finally saying, "No I'm not."

"What's going on?"

"Where do I start?"

"Where'd you go? Who were those guys that just came and took you?"

She shakes her head and looks up at the ceiling for a moment, as if she doesn't want to think about it. She takes another sip.

"And when did you change? I was at your apartment."

"Look—it's a long story. I got away from those guys for the moment. Does it really matter?"

You're confused but more than that you're once again mesmerized by her smile and her lips and her cheekbones and those eyes and all you can do is shake your head.

"Are you okay?" she asks, coming next to you and wrapping her arms around you.

You don't resist. You're too tired and too sore and too bewildered to resist the contact.

"What happened at my apartment?"

"We got there and Amanda was showing me around and your ex—or someone—was waiting in your bedroom closet. He had something—a small bat or something like that—and just like that I was out. I woke up and he was gone and so was Amanda."

"Did you—what'd you do? Did you call the cops?"

You shake your head. "No. I just—I don't know. I was the one who hit him in the club. I'm not—"

"It's fine. Really."

Jasmine still stands beside you and rubs the back of your head as though you're a child.

You suddenly feel a lot more awake.

"You don't know what happened to Amanda?" she asks.

"No."

"I wouldn't be surprised if Riley came here looking for me."

"Look—I don't know—what exactly happened? Where did you go?"

"Those guys who showed up at 345. They're just—I know them and they're fine. Just—look, I can't get into it now, but it's okay. Things are okay."

"Somebody shoved a gun in my face and dropped me off in the Bronx tonight."

Jasmine sits back down and takes a drink from her martini glass. The comment doesn't exactly shock her the way you thought it would.

"Literally?" she asks.

"Yeah. A lot of people seem to be looking for you."

She shakes her head, looks back at the stairwell where she came from, then finishes her drink.

"Well, you win the prize."

"What prize?"

"You found me."

"That's fine, but—"

She stands and takes your hand and urges you up.

"We're dancing."

Anyone watching would look at you and your puppy eyes and wagging tail and shake his head in disgust. No explanation about the men and going missing and calling in fear and then showing up here untouched in new clothes and oblivious to everything.

She just doesn't have one care in the world.

And for tonight, for now, you sorta like that. You want that attitude to rub off on you.

You want to walk forward without baggage weighing you down. Without a care in the world. Without the burden of responsibilities.

So you follow her. No more explanations necessary.

3:36 A.M.

THE MUSIC IS ALMOST LOUD ENOUGH to overpower your mind, to not let you think of anything else.

Almost.

But some things are stronger than volume and liquor and even mad desire.

Memories. Branded on your heart and your soul.

And you think back to the most unlikely of memories to come visit you in this New York club named Exit.

For a brief second, you remember holding her.

When you held her in your arms, you believed that everything in the world would change. That everything was okay. And that regardless of what happened, things would work out. Life had meaning.

You named her Olivia.

Her cheeks were silk and her lips were so tiny and so original. She had soft dark hair and Lisa's features in miniature. Hands that fit in your palm. A tiny voice that could still belt out tears. And the most precious and adorable face you'd ever seen.

You were smitten, you were in love, and you believed that you couldn't love anything more than your daughter at this moment.

And things did change.

Olivia changed everything, as did Peyton.

And things with Lisa got better. You saw her in a different light, a different context.

But even all of this couldn't prevent life and its busyness from creeping in.

From life and its lure drawing you closer.

From your own self and your own weaknesses.

You're sacrificing it all—for what? For what?

What are you doing, Michael?

You know better.

You know so much better.

But you keep going.

What is it about you that doesn't have the *stop* button? What is it about this night and this woman you're following onto the dance floor?

3:37 A.M.

THIS MUSIC IS DESIGNED for people looking for people. The beat propels you forward and the music incites feeling and emotion. Simple straightforward lyrics like "I will surrender" and "burning with desire" and "watch you fade away" and endless, ridiculous words about needing and wanting and hoping all make you think that you truly want and need the woman dancing across from you. Jasmine's long legs and arms sway and turn and twist in suggestive poses and for the moment you don't care how ridiculous you look.

The memory of Olivia evaporates in the swarm of dancing fools around you.

A couple of hours ago someone was shoving a gun in your face because of this woman. Then somebody knocked you out. Now you're at a club with her.

And for some crazy reason it seems justified.

"I can't let you go," the voice sings, with the chiming trance music following.

You see men looking at Jasmine and checking her out. She seems oblivious and takes your hand and smiles at your reluctance. She slides and slithers up to you and bounces back and forth. Her blonde hair whips behind her and you move and let yourself go.

One song passes and the room seems to turn and twirl around you.

You find yourself moving with Jasmine. She's as tall as you are with her heels.

"If you could read my mind," a woman's voice sings.

Jasmine raises her eyebrows and you laugh at the insanity of this. The utter craziness of this.

"Should I turn and walk away?" the singer asks.

But you're staying.

You're an absolute idiot.

But staring at the face and the smile, it doesn't matter. Nothing matters.

A new Madonna song comes on and you wonder how long Madonna can continue to release music. You were going to clubs when Madonna was fresh and hip, and she's still making everybody dance and gyrate on the dance floor.

The song ignites Jasmine and she moves away from you

and shakes her head and moves her body to the beat. You watch her as she is lost in her own world.

When the song ends, she comes up to you with a glistening forehead.

"I need to use the ladies room," she says. "I'll be right back."

You nod, then add, "I'll come with you."

She leaves the dance floor and starts downstairs, then notices that you're following.

"I don't need a chaperone," she says as she licks her lips.

"Yeah, but maybe I do."

She laughs. "I'll be fine. Seriously."

You reach the bottom of the stairwell and she stands there, annoyed that you're still following her.

"Just wait here, okay?"

"I just don't—This place is huge."

"It's fine. I'll be right back."

You watch her descend another set of stairs that have signs for the restroom. A funky, wild song comes out of the door you're next to. You meander into a glowing, red-and-orange-lighted room with a whole assortment of characters dancing and laughing. The bar is lit up and the bartender is laughing and asks you what you want. You order something and then drink the cocktail and wait for Jasmine and watch the crowd.

You don't feel like Michael anymore. You feel like someone else who doesn't have a name or a face or an identity.

The drink feels good going down.

And you wait and listen to three more songs before you
place your empty glass on the bar and decide to go find
Jasmine.

Not again.

You no longer hear that voice saying *You know better.*

3:51 A.M.

YOU'RE IN THE RESTROOM WASHING your hands and listening to the animated beat outside. You look in the mirror and see someone standing behind you.

He's staring right at you.

You go to get a paper towel and the guy blocks your way.

"Excuse me," you say.

He wears a black sports coat and jeans. He's your size with a thick mustache and dark eyes.

"Someone wants to talk with you," he says, his eyes unwavering.

"Who's that?"

"Why don't you come with me?"

"I don't think so," you say, starting to walk around him.

You feel an arm wrap itself around your neck, and suddenly

you can't breathe. It's strong and quick and you think *God what am I thinking what is he doing* and then someone breathless and sweaty comes to the open doorway to the bathroom.

"Get out!" the man holding you in a brace shouts, along with a few expletives.

The young sweaty club hopper turns around instantly.

"Either I drag you upstairs or you go on your own," he whispers in your ear.

You're beginning to black out and you nod, not able to say anything, not able to breathe.

He lets you go and you fall to your knees, gasping, choking.

"Get up," he says, oblivious to the fact that he almost crushed the life out of you.

You nod and hold up a hand and keep coughing. You stand and feel wobbly and start to go get something to drink, but the guy pushes you and tells you to move.

Outside the men's restroom, you half expect to see Jasmine waiting in the hallway at the bottom of the wide stairs. But she's not there.

Thank God.

"Keep going up," he tells you.

You walk up the stairs as music continues to dance and beat around you and strangers pass by oblivious.

"What's this about?" you ask over your shoulder.

"Shut your face and keep walking."

You pass a man dressed in black pants and a black dress

shirt who looks like he could bench-press you. The guy nods at the man behind you.

Where do these Herculean guys come from and what do they really think? Do they get hired to look tough and act like pieces of meat?

They're doing a great job.

You wonder if Jasmine is going to come back.

Maybe I should leave before she does.

A couple passes by laughing hysterically and having what looks like the night of their life.

Why couldn't that be Jasmine and me? Laughing and drunk with no cares and no responsibilities?

You reach the top of the stairs and a man stands there sizing you up.

"It's okay," the guy behind you says. "Second door on the left."

You look behind and see that the man who strangled you is being accompanied by the big guy in all black.

You cough again.

Your head still hurts.

Your mouth is like cotton from the alcohol you've drunk.

Your heart is hung out to dry.

You wonder where Jasmine disappeared to.

Again.

"Go on in," the guy tells you.

You open the door, unsure who you'll meet, unsure what this is all about.

This is all your own fault, Michael.

4:08 A.M.

IT'S 4:08 A.M. AND LISA IS PROBABLY DEEP into her sleep and Olivia and Peyton are in their beds tucked away and breathing sweetly and silently.

Meanwhile you're standing in a room that looks like a small VIP lounge with several couches and glass coffee tables positioned throughout. Strange artwork with naked women in various provocative poses adorns the dark room with moody canned lighting. You notice a man sitting on the white couch, smoking a cigarette and watching you.

"Come on in," he says in a calm voice.

You walk over to the couch and sit in a leather loveseat next to it. The door is closed but you can still hear the music from below.

"I don't know what this is all about," you rush to say.

The man looks to be in his forties. He has dark features and could be Cuban. He has thinning hair and a heavy five o'clock shadow. He wears light pants and a suit coat with a colorful shirt.

He doesn't react to your comment. He continues smoking his cigarette and just watches you.

"What is your name?" he asks in a voice that has a tinge of an accent, tempered by years of living in the States.

"Michael."

"Michael what?"

"What is this all about?"

He smiles. "Ms. Shreve says you have something for me."

You look at the man and in the dim glow of the lights of this room, you notice a scar on the edge of his neck. It looks like it came from a knife.

"She told you I have what?"

"To make things even. To square things away."

The man looks at you, watching, waiting. You wonder if he blinks at all.

The guy who strangled you and the big guy in black are probably out in the hallway waiting. They're just a call away.

"I don't know what you're talking about."

The man nods without expression.

"I keep taking the young lady at her word. It's becoming a little difficult to continue to do that."

"What do you think I have?"

He ignores the question.

"I would hate for something to happen to Ms. Shreve."

"Where is she?" you demand.

"Please, no need to raise your voice."

The man puts out his cigarette and then rests his arms on his legs, staring at you.

"What is a guy like you doing involved with something like this?"

"Something like what?"

He doesn't believe your earnestness, but looks amused at the fact that you're trying.

"You know, all I need is a name," the man says. "Then your life is ours."

You think of your license in your wallet.

No way is anybody touching me.

Nobody is going to find out who I am.

"Whatever is going on, it's none of my business."

"This is your business. I think you know that."

You stand up, wanting to get away from feeling like you're in trouble, like you're being interrogated.

"Where is she?" you ask.

"I think you know that better than I do."

"I just saw her a few moments ago."

"Of course you did. Why else did you come here?"

You look at him and he acts as though he's spoken with you a hundred times before.

"I don't know what—"

"Please now. This is not worth the effort."

"What effort? What are you talking about? I just met her tonight."

"Did the plan change?"

You stare at him and shake your head.

"I don't know what you're talking about," you say in the most earnest voice you can utter.

"You being here means something, and I know that."

"Yeah, well, maybe I just want to leave."

"You can't do that."

He takes out a cigarette from the pack in his coat and starts smoking it. He doesn't look bothered or worried in the least.

"I don't know what this is about or what's going on with you and 'Ms. Shreve,' and I think that it's none of my business."

"It's only business," the man says. "That's all."

"Yeah, but it's not mine."

"Where are you from?" he asks.

You look at the door and then back at him.

"You're not from around here, are you?"

He inhales the cigarette and blows out the smoke. He seems okay at your reticence.

"It doesn't matter if you leave this club or this city. I have ways of finding people."

"This is not my business."

For the first time all night you feel like Lisa and the kids could be pulled into this mess, that they could actually be in serious danger.

It's not just about you and a pretty stranger anymore.

This is your family they're talking about.

They don't know my name.

All you have to do is get out of here. Somehow get out of here without their knowing anything more about you.

Jasmine knows your name.

But she doesn't know your whole name, does she?

"Uh uh uh," he starts to say as you turn for the door. "You don't want to do that."

"Do what?"

"Open that door."

You look at the man as he takes a long draw from his cigarette. He grins and shows teeth in bad need of repair.

"Maybe I want to," you say.

"And maybe there are fifty guys in this place who don't really want you to leave. It won't be my problem if you leave this room. It will be their problem."

"Oh yeah?"

"Yes. And you don't want it to be their problem. You want it to be my problem. With me, things stay calm. Things stay safe."

"Look, man—"

The man curses at you and you begin to wonder if he's going to do something instead of just sit.

"Don't call me *man*," he says.

This is a decision point. Stay in here with this little calm guy or go outside

to what?

and risk something.

Nothing about life is ever safe. Every breath and every decision and every second is a risk.

This is no longer about me and about the woman named Jasmine. This is about my family tucked away safely in Deerfield, Illinois.

"Why don't you stay and talk for a few more moments. Be rational."

You breathe in and look around and then know that there is only one thing you can do.

"See ya, *man*," you say right before opening the door and sprinting outside.

4:17 A.M.

HE STANDS A DOZEN YARDS AWAY from the door, close to the wall. A towering figure of black, unmovable. You don't think but simply run at him, doing your best linebacker impression, steadying your shoulder for the dig into his gut. But it feels like barging into a statue. The man barely moves while you feel your shoulder crunch and sense a tight pain and then go bouncing off to the side. The man curses and for a minute looks like a bull being charged by a Chihuahua, as if he's wondering *What in the world are you even trying to do?*

You roll to one side and get back on your feet. You glance at him and see a hand going to his side.

You don't stick around to see what he's grabbing for.

Where's Jasmine?

The hallway is dimly lit and you don't notice the other guy coming your way. All you want to do is find the stairs.

As you gain your balance, something slams against your back and sends you flying.

You manage to fall on your knees and your hands. Somehow you get back up and turn around just in time to see the man who got you in the armlock down in the bathroom.

Not this time.

Fear and adrenaline rush through your body and are almost so thick that you can taste them. You see the guy coming at you and grab him by his collar with your left hand, slamming your right fist against his cheek.

You punch him in the jaw once, then in the forehead, then in the ear. You punch several more times and feel his body go limp.

He didn't see it coming. He didn't see those punches in me.

As he falls down, you turn around and begin running. You know the big guy in black is coming after you.

You find the large staircase and bolt down it, sending a half-drunk bystander sprawling down the stairs. If only you could have done that to the bruiser back there. You turn and continue down another flight of steps, heading to where you last saw Jasmine.

A quick glance upstairs reveals the man in black coming toward you like a robot. He's in no hurry.

You get to the hallway and run past an open doorway that

has a picture of a woman on it. You back up and go inside. A lady sitting on a stool looks at you without surprise. She's listening to a boom box and sits beside a counter full of gum, cigarettes, perfume, and various items of makeup and hairspray.

"There a blonde in here?"

"Lots of blondes in here," the lady says, talking ten times slower than you.

"Now. Like right now?"

"Everything okay?" she asks.

"No. She came in here about fifteen minutes ago."

"Nobody's in here now."

You turn and look toward the stairs.

"You sure?"

She nods and you go rushing out, away from the stairs and into one of the main rooms that has blasting hip-hop music. The dance floor is crowded with couples all moving to the beat and blending in to the vibrant yellows and reds from the lights.

You try to scan the room but it's impossible.

Forget Jasmine.

But a part of you can't. A part of you won't.

I'm getting out of here.

You're going to call him Johnny Cash, the man in black who stands by the door. He scans the room and finds you.

In his hand watch what's in his hand.

It's not a gun. It's a phone or a walkie-talkie.

You scan the room for somewhere else to go. Wall, wall, bar—

There it is.

Another open entryway leads to who-knows-what.

A man in a white T-shirt and jeans stands there, looking your way. He's not as big as Johnny Cash, but he looks mean. Chiseled arms. You're not going to be able to punch him five or six times.

You have no other choice.

You meander around the dancers and then stop several people away from the new guy. He's coming toward you.

You take the hand of a woman dancing by herself. You pull her to you, then bring her over toward the doorway. It's after four and she's good to go and she laughs as you mock dance with her.

Stopping in front of the guy in the white T-shirt, you hand her off to him and start sprinting again. The guy lets go of the woman and follows after you.

You pass a bar with half a dozen television screens. This is where Jasmine first found you, where she held you in her arms. A set of stairs, smaller, go off to the side. As you ascend them, you hear steps behind you. A guy calls out after you and curses.

Another floor up, you continue sprinting and find the main dance hall of the club. Only three people dance, the music still jamming and the lights still flickering.

I got to get out of here.

You suck in breaths and feel the ache in your side.

You pause for a moment, then go back to the main area where the stairs are.

Your cell phone vibrates against your leg.

You continue up the main flight of steps. You must be on the second floor now. The music is different up here, more industrial and loud and violent. The dance floor is smaller and fuller.

You try to lose yourself in the crowd but it doesn't work.

White T-shirt guy walks to where you are. He's holding something to his side.

He approaches you and looks at you, motioning you to come with him.

In his hand is a gun. A small handgun, but very real.

You're not going anywhere, his look says.

He grins, thinking that the gun gives him total control.

He doesn't realize who he's got cornered. A rabid dog who will do anything to get out of here.

Anything.

Your hand goes toward his forearm. You find yourself trying to wrestle the gun away from him. Somehow you can't believe your own strength.

Fear.

You jerk and fight with the guy and it looks like the two of you are involved in some violent, brutal dance.

The music and crowd and the guy's biceps and the jerking result in a loud shot that stuns everyone for a millisecond, then sends everybody in a panic.

You send an elbow into the man's gut. You hear him suck in air in pain as he drops the gun.

Pick it up pick it up.

People tear past you but all you can see is the gun on the floor.

Pick it up before it's too late Mike pick it up.

Someone's foot sends the gun sliding across the floor.

You follow it and then dive to try and get it.

Somehow your hand finds the pistol. You pick it up and then get back on your legs and follow the crowd out of the club.

Halfway down the flight of stairs, you see the man in black.

Watching. And waiting.

People are tearing by you, a few women screaming. You decide to go with the crowd.

Watch it.

As you get closer to the man, standing there, waiting, you look over the banister.

Use the gun use the gun it's time to use the gun.

The main entryway to the club is just below. People are streaming into it from three ways trying to get out. A gunshot in a club might not be a common thing, but people have an idea what they need to do when they hear it.

You go to the edge of the stairs and hop on the banister. You climb over the railing and then lean your body off, dropping the rest of the way. You make sure you don't drop the gun.

You land on your feet. Hard.

As you go to run, something doesn't feel right. Your left foot stings and you go hopping on it, following the stream of people.

He's after you and you know it. He probably has a gun.

So do you.

He probably knows how to use it.

What he wants—what they want—you're not thinking of that now.

You follow the crowd and feel trapped in the mass of bodies and almost get tripped up but finally you feel the coolness of the night, seeing the people standing around and looking panicked and confused.

You're not sure where you are or where Jasmine is.

Taking out your cell phone, you look to see the missed call. A New York number.

There's no time for listening to a voice mail. The taxi you asked to wait around is long gone. You head down a sidewalk, the darkest one you can spot, hoping to find a cab or the entryway to the subway.

Your left ankle is tender and feels like it could give way any minute.

You look behind you and around you to see if you're being followed.

You keep walking down the street, trying to get far away from this club.

The gun in your hand feels oddly comforting.

4:37 A.M.

STEPS LEAD DOWN TO THE SUBWAY. You keep turning around, afraid someone is following you, afraid someone will catch up and stop you from going any further.

You descend the stairs and feel your ankle ache. Trying to sprint anymore tonight will be pointless.

At least you have the gun. It's resting against your gut tucked in your jeans.

At the bottom of the steps, a narrow graffiti-marked hallway leads to an open area where machines let you buy tickets. You purchase one, not sure where you're going, not sure you even care.

As you hold the plastic card in your hand, you decide to check the voice mail.

Don't do it.

Maybe you're tired and still a little buzzed and not thinking on full capacity. But night has almost turned to day and what are you going to do?

You're still worried about Jasmine.

You press *play*.

The voice, of course, is Jasmine's. Frantic but muffled. Talking very slowly.

"Michael. He took me—Riley came and he's a crazy man. I've never seen him like this. I tried—I didn't know what else to do—he made us go back to my place. He hit me. I'm scared, Michael. He stepped out for a minute, but he's coming back and I'm scared of what he's going to do—what he's going to make me do."

She pauses, then speaks deliberately, in a whisper. "Please come. Please help me."

You ask the guy at the information counter how to get to Jasmine's address in the Village. He gives you a few directions and tells you which stop to get off at. Your mind has always been good that way. Someone tells you something—instructions, directions—just once, and you get it.

You know where to go when someone gives you directions. Wandering around on your own—that's when you get into trouble.

The subway is surprisingly occupied with people and once again, you wonder when this town sleeps. If this town sleeps.

You sit and rest and listen to the tracks click underneath you and the sound of strangers talking in muffled, tired tones.

The cold hard light makes you feel sleepy. You sit and wonder what you're doing.

You take a deep breath, in and out, in and out. Your heart is just slowing down.

This isn't a television show. This is real and it's your life and you feel the adrenaline still coursing through your body.

You work on a laptop and deal with numbers and theories and salesmen and women and you've never been shot at before.

How many people can claim they've been shot at?

The doors open at a stop. You look around the cabin of the train. A couple sit holding hands looking as though they've had a long night and that night is coming to a close. A homeless guy sleeps in a corner. An African-American man looks as though he's on his way to work. A young lady looks like a tourist.

Then you see the well-dressed Asian guy, looking your way, not hesitating when you glance at him.

For a moment you think it's the guy who held a gun to your face in the back of the town car. But it's not.

This guy is wearing a coat and looks wide awake and sits in a seat close by.

When did you get on?

You can't remember seeing him get on, but you didn't pay much attention right after you first stepped on here and sat down.

Was he at the club?

Which club, another voice asks you.

You don't know why the man at the club was interrogating you. Why the men picked you up and drove you to the middle of nowhere. And why an ex-boyfriend has seemed hell-bent on finding Jasmine tonight and making life miserable for you.

You know exactly why.

It's the weakness of men like yourself and others everywhere. A woman like Jasmine—she is rare indeed.

Outwardly.

Yes, you don't know anything about her. She's confident and enticing but you don't *really* know her, do you?

Can a gorgeous face and body have this sort of effect on a man like you?

The train passes in the night and you feel the jerking motion and close your eyes for a second. You can see Jasmine's lips, her long hair, eyes that move and melt you.

You are that weak. You know it. You can admit it, here, early in the morning, in the train car heading back to a stranger's apartment.

She might be in trouble.

And you might be too, another voice says. Why risk it?

Risk what?

You picture Lisa and Olivia and Peyton. The home and the family and the life you've spent so long trying to build, that you have helped build, that should be standing firm.

A firm foundation.

You wonder if that's what you have. Have you ever had a firm foundation? What does that saying really, truly mean?

The song about building your house on the sand or on the stone—is it stone, what is it again?—runs through your mind.

How could you throw it all away just for

for what?

a night with a beautiful woman?

You gotta get perspective.

The Asian man with the chiseled jaw hasn't stopped looking at you, watching you, almost waiting. He has remarkably pale skin, flawless in its complexion.

What am I doing?

You've asked yourself this question a hundred times. A sinking, clawing feeling rips open your inside. You can feel your heart beating.

Turn around.

You don't know what's out there when you get off this train. What's up those steps and out on those streets and in that high-rise.

Trouble.

But the stop comes and you stand up, your ankle burning.

You step off. For a moment, nobody is around you.

Then you see him twenty yards away, the well-dressed stranger who has been staring at you for some time.

Do I run?

You can't run and you know it. You turn around and start heading out, up stairs that you have to ascend slowly.

The man is lagging behind.

You pick up the pace and finally get to a flat surface.

He is stopped, talking on his cell phone or checking it for messages.

You start walking faster, trying to get out of here.

You turn around once, twice, one more time, but the man is nowhere to be seen.

On the street, you breathe in fresh morning air and exhale and wait to see if the stranger is still following you.

Nothing. For several minutes, you're alone on a corner of a street in New York.

Your heart is pounding. Your ankle aching. And your gut trembling.

Yet you still keep walking.

You're afraid of leaving this night not knowing if this strange woman you've met is in danger.

4:45 A.M.

THERE'S SOMETHING YOU WANT and something you need. Something you've wanted and needed for a while. Yet you've never been able to articulate it, never even been able to acknowledge its gnawing little presence. It's an assurance. A validation. A meaning and a hope and something else, something more, something.

Every day there is a list waiting for you. Names and faces and voices all wanting and needing an answer. There are the clients and the numbers and the contacts and the calls. There are the deals and the deeds and the deadlines and the decisions. And sometimes you want—you need—a break.

The hard-nosed men and women in today's business world deal with this daily, and some can't take it. Some remain medicated one way or the other. Others you know say they rely on God. It makes you feel worse because sometimes you try—God knows you try—but it doesn't seem like enough.

God's been very silent for a while.

Maybe I've been silent back.

It's morning and this busy city suddenly seems deserted. You hear the sound of your shoes hitting the pavement, feel the weight of each step. Your feet hurt, strained from walking and running all night.

There needs to be a change. Something in you needs to change. Maybe this job and this life but perhaps it doesn't have to be so dramatic. Maybe you can start in the small areas of your life. Small steps.

Maybe you need to celebrate what you have instead of wanting what you don't have.

Your mother's smile and sweet innocence come to mind in the darkness of the city street. You remember when she used to know you, when she wasn't battling this crippling and cruel disease. When she loved and protected you even though you couldn't protect her.

You can't save her. No matter what you do, you can't do a thing for her.

The thought makes you angry and you know whom your anger is directed toward.

Why are you doing this to me? Why?

You're about ready to have another one-way conversation when you hear somebody behind you.

You turn around.

It's the guy from the train. The well-dressed Asian guy. He's on the sidewalk walking toward you.

Without thinking about it, you grasp the handgun and point it at him. You walk toward him and see his expression of shock and surprise.

"What do you want?" you shout out.

"Nothing."

"What are you doing then?"

"It's okay. Really. It's okay. I was just making sure—"

"Making sure what?" you shout as you wave the gun at his head.

"Making sure where you're going."

"I'm having a bad night and I swear at this point I don't care if I use this thing."

"Look, it's fine, it's okay. Seriously. I'm not going to do anything. I work for Jana. For her parents."

"What?"

"I'm just making sure Jana is okay."

"Do you know where she is?"

"I was supposed to keep tabs on you."

"Why?"

The gun in your hand seems like a play toy. You're playing cops and robbers.

Which one are you?

"I just do what I'm asked to do."

"Where is Jana?"

"I don't know. I swear I don't know. Please. Put down the gun."

"Then stop following me."

"Okay, fine. No problem."

The guy sounds weak and desperate and you feel sorry for him.

I understand what you're feeling.

"Is Jana home?"

"I told you, I don't know."

"Are you from that club?"

"What do you mean?"

The guy looks confused and itching to run away.

"Just take off. And tell whoever you're working for to leave me alone. I swear."

He nods and starts to back away.

"Go on," you shout out.

He sprints away and you find it odd to see a guy in dress slacks and dress shoes sprinting down a New York street.

What next?

One more stop. Jana's apartment. Or Jasmine's.

One more opportunity to see if she's okay.

You have to make sure she's okay.

You can do that one thing.

You owe it to her. You don't even know why, but you do.

You look at the gun in your hand, and the picture seems

odd. You feel like you did back at the clubs, like a stranger, an imposter trying to play out someone else's life.

You're not going to use that.

But you stick it in your jeans just to have it. Just in case . . .

Just in case.

4:57 A.M.

THE WORLD IS WAKING UP. Part of you just wants to close your eyes and rest. But your body feels electric and you're out of breath as you enter the building. There is a different doorman now, but you go up to him and tell him your business.

"I'm here to see Jana Shreve."

He nods and puts the call in. After a second, he waves you onto the elevator.

You wait at the door, the shiny ceramic tile showing your reflection. The metal doors open and you walk into the small elevator.

You press floor eight.

God help me help me through this protect me Lord.

Does God listen to the prayers of an idiot? Of a deliberate

sinner? Of someone walking the wrong path and knowingly
going on?

We all walk the wrong path.

The elevator is quiet and the doors soon open.

Your legs are heavy, your ankle throbbing. You find the
door you're looking for and knock.

Who knows what's behind the door.

You hear nothing, so you knock again.

And wait.

Then you try the door. It opens without a sound.

You step inside, the floor creaking and causing you to
stop for the moment. The lights are all on, as they were when
you left the apartment. You see a coat resting over the sofa.

Faint voices come from the bedroom.

What are they doing?

You walk near the kitchen. The voices are casual. You hear
a laugh.

So now what?

You take in the apartment you left hours ago. Nothing
looks different. But somehow it *feels* different. You no longer
look at everything with shades of mystique covering it. You are
tired and want to go home and want to make sure Jasmine is
okay.

You step into the main room next to the couch.

The talking stops.

You stand there and wait, unsure of what to do or where

to go. You feel the gun at your side but keep it tucked in, secure.

You hear footsteps. You look up and see Riley walking toward you wearing jeans and a T-shirt.

He stops and stares for a second, letting go a loud questioning curse.

"What the—What do you think you're doing?"

You don't move and don't hesitate.

"Where's Jasmine?"

His head points to the bedroom he just came from.

"Jasmine?" you shout out.

"Who let you in?" Riley asks.

"Where's Jasmine? And what are you doing here?"

The man laughs. "What do you mean, what am *I* doing here?"

There is a slight cut at the bridge of his nose.

"Jasmine!" you shout again.

Riley points a finger at you and his eyes tighten. "I'll tell you this one time and one time only. If you don't get out of here, so help me God, I'm gonna—"

"Mike."

The tall figure that steps into the room is holding a gun and aiming it at Riley.

"J, what the—"

"Get away from me!" Jasmine says, walking around him to get to you.

The smug grin on Riley's face is gone, his curly hair messed up. He looks bewildered.

"What are you doing with that, J?" he asks.

Jasmine comes to your side, still holding the gun at Riley. Her eyes are dark and teary. Her hair is up and she's still in the jeans and camisole top she was wearing earlier.

What were they doing?

A shot of anger courses through you.

Am I jealous?

Her long velvet arms surround you as she hugs you. She keeps the gun pointed at Riley.

"Help me, Michael."

"It's okay," you whisper in her ear, your stomach dropping and tightening. "Give me the gun."

She smells so good it's not right for a woman this hot to smell so good.

You don't want to let go. You want to feel her silky hair against your cheek, feel her body against yours. But she pulls away.

"Are you okay?"

She shakes her head and shoots a look of disgust Riley's way. You look at her and see the bruise on her forehead.

"Did he do that?"

She nods, her eyes still on him, her hand holding the small black automatic.

"Do what?" Riley says.

"Shut your face," Jasmine says.

"Jasmine, give me the gun," you tell her.

"No."

"What are you doing, J? Where'd you get that thing?"

"Stay right there," you tell Riley.

He starts to walk toward you, and Jasmine waves the gun around with reckless abandon.

"I swear, don't you come near me. Don't you *touch* me."

Riley stops and puts a hand out in front of his face.

"Give me that," you tell Jasmine.

You slowly walk behind her. Her hand is shaking.

Riley curses at both of you, saying she's not about to use that.

"You just watch me," Jasmine says.

"Please, give me the gun," you say. You touch her shoulder, then her arm, then put your hand on the gun.

"It's okay," you tell her. "Let's just—come on—let's call the cops."

"No. Not the cops—I can't. I don't want my name in the papers."

"Call the cops for what?"

You finally have the gun in your hand. You keep it pointed at Riley.

"Stay right there," you bark out, stopping Riley from moving anymore.

Maybe he finally realizes you're serious. Maybe seeing the

gun in your hands means something else. He puts his arms up at his head level.

"Man, she's doing a number on your head."

Jasmine screams out a few curses at him. You have to hold her back from attacking him.

"What are you even babbling on about?" he asks. "We were just about to—you were the one that called me!"

"He's a liar," Jasmine tells you. "He's been after me all night and found me at the club and made me come back here."

Riley looks at her, confused and a bit amused.

"You're making this up as you go," he says.

"Just stay there," you tell him.

"Man, this is not your concern."

"You made it my concern."

"And why's that?" Riley asks.

"Because you beat up on women," you say.

Riley's dark eyes look curious, amused. "Oh, you think I did that?"

"Who else would?"

"I can give you a list, buddy. I'm telling you." He stops, shaking his head. "Man, you have no idea what you're getting into."

"Who else did this?"

"Why don't you tell your new protector who did that?"

"You did," Jasmine says, standing right behind you, her hand locked onto your arm.

"You're mental," Riley says. "That chick's a head case. Seriously. You got problems, J. Big problems. I thought you needed me tonight."

"What are you doing here?" you ask.

"She called me! Man, stop pointing that gun in my face."

"You didn't happen to be here earlier? Waiting?"

"For what?"

Riley's doing a great job acting, looking both angry and confused at the same time.

"Waiting for Jasmine. And when she didn't show up, you knocked me unconscious."

Riley looks at Jasmine for a moment, as though he can't believe what he's hearing. He takes it all in and for a moment, just thinks. He steps a bit closer.

"Stay right there," you order him.

He holds his hands at shoulder level. "I'm not going to do a thing."

"Then stay there."

"What are you—oh man, you're seriously crazy. I just got here after she called me—"

"That's a lie," Jasmine says.

"And after I was at the club. Trying to repair my busted nose."

"You deserved that busted nose," you say.

"Yeah, but you're the one going around trying to—I don't know. Trying to protect someone you don't even know."

"I know what you've done to her."

"What?"

"Riley, you know it's true," Jasmine says.

You stand on the edge of the main room, a couch separating Riley and you, Jasmine behind you. Riley begins to back up, his hands looking as if they're trying to wave you and your gun down.

"This is crazy."

"Stop," you say as Riley walks away. "You're not going anywhere."

"What do you want? J, we're through."

"Good."

"No, I mean we are *so* through. You're nothing but a pretty, rich whore."

"Shut your mouth," you say.

"Why don't you make me," he says, cursing.

"Shoot him," Jasmine says.

You look at her and see the serious expression on her face. Riley is stunned as well.

"Shoot him. It's self-defense. He broke in here—"

"I didn't break in here!"

"—I told him to give me back his key but he had another made. He came in here to rape me."

Riley's eyes are large and his head shakes. "That's nonsense, man. Does she look like I touched her?"

"You've had too much to drink tonight. You know exactly why you came over here."

"Yeah, you called me, you stupid tramp."

"I said shut your mouth," you tell Riley.

"And I said why don't you make me."

"Shoot him."

You think of the knock on your head and then the bruise on Jasmine's face.

Protect her. Don't let something else happen to her.

The gun in your hand starts to feel heavy.

"Do it, Michael. Do it for me."

You look at her and see the earnest expression on her face. Something about it scares you.

"Jasmine, I . . ."

"He's going to keep coming back. Do you know what it's like? Do you know how it feels to live in fear?"

Yeah, you sorta do.

Riley curses. "She's so full of—"

"Just shut up."

"Come on, man, you're tired. You're tired and out of your mind. Just put the gun down."

"Don't do it, Michael. Don't. Don't let him sweet-talk you."

Riley takes a step toward you, and you hold the gun more firmly. "Back off."

"I'm telling you, man, you're making a big mistake."

The man in the T-shirt and designer jeans looks at you with questioning, annoyed eyes. He still doesn't think you can do it.

"Help me," Jasmine tells you.

She comes up behind you and slips a hand on your chest, rubbing it.

"Please, Mike. Please help me."

It's not like it looks in the movies. This doesn't feel right or normal.

What am I doing here?

"Do it. Just do it."

Riley starts to curse and you feel Jasmine's touch and your mind is twirling and your body aches and your hand shakes and you think about it. For just a split second, you think about it.

Then you see the gun in your hand, the second gun that night, and realize that the picture is wrong, that this is all so very wrong.

Instead of aiming the gun, you let your hand fall to your side.

"Mike!" Jasmine says.

"Get out of here," you tell Riley.

"That's what I was trying to do."

Jasmine looks at you in disbelief.

"No."

"It's okay," you tell her.

"No, it's not!"

"It's fine. We're fine."

"Please, Mike. Please . . ."

You look over at Jasmine. She gives you sad, sexy eyes.

The gun stays down, resting at your side.

"Let's go," you tell her.

She breathes in and looks at you, then back at Riley.

"What about him?"

"I'm calling the cops."

"No, don't do that," she demands.

Riley is nodding his head, hands still up. "I'm just—I'm out of here, okay? No problem. J, everything's cool. Fine. I can just—look here, it's fine, seriously."

He's putting his jacket back on.

"Don't let him go."

You look at Jasmine and want to reach out and touch her soft face. "I can't kill a man."

"Yes, you can. It's easy."

You shake your head and grip the gun. "I can't."

Something on her face changes. A look of disgust.

Is that directed at me or at Riley?

But as you stare at her, the door opens and shuts and Riley is gone.

"He'll be back," she says.

"Then let's get out of here."

"Where to?"

"I don't know. Let's—let's go back to my hotel room."

She stares at you for a moment, and her mouth goes to say something, then she stops herself and nods and walks to her bedroom.

Your whole body shudders and you place the gun down on the kitchen counter, toss the other gun from your jeans right next to it, then rush over to the sink and start to heave. You don't have much inside of you to vomit—you did that earlier.

You finally stop and turn on the water and take several large gulps of it. Then you run the faucet over your face and your forehead.

You were aiming a gun at a stranger, close to pulling the trigger.

I wouldn't have done it.

But you could have. Accidentally. If Riley had charged at you. Or if Jasmine had somehow gotten her hands on it. What would have happened if

don't think about it

you had killed somebody?

And now.

Yes, and now.

You don't want to think anymore.

Riley is gone. And soon you will be too.

5:23 A.M.

IN THE COLD, FAKE-LEATHER BACKSEAT of the rushing cab, Jasmine puts a hand on your leg, then moves it up to find your hand.

"Thank you," she says.

You nod and look at her and see the lights and the whirl of the city pass behind her.

Her face looks young and scared and needy.

She looks at you for a long time, holding your hand, pressing it, beckoning you to come closer.

You feel a shiver go through your body.

The look stays. She's waiting, wondering what's taking you so long, wondering why you haven't already made a move.

Your body feels electric even though your heart and soul know this is wrong.

This is so wrong so wrong so absolutely wrong but it feels right and feels like I want it.

You begin to move closer to her. She looks at your lips.

She can tell you're afraid.

"Everything is going to be okay," she says.

And you put your arms around her and hold her in your arms.

The world passes by. If only everything could stop and be put on hold and you could just stay here in her arms.

Just a minute ago you were seconds away from killing a man.

The thought terrifies you.

Another part of you knows you let her down.

I was afraid.

You feel her body close to yours.

I'm still afraid.

"Here we go," the driver says as the cab comes to a stop.

You keep looking at Jasmine, then force a smile and give the guy a twenty.

You open the door and watch Jasmine climb out. She stands and looks at the hotel building.

"Times Square, huh?"

"Nice when you don't have to pay for it," you say.

"Are we going up?"

"Come on."

You lead her through the lobby and to an elevator.

You press your floor number. The inches that separate the

two of you almost seem awkward, unnecessary.

Jasmine moves closer to you.

You take her hand in yours again. "You're going to be okay."

"Sure about that?" she asks.

"Yes."

"I know a way I can be very okay."

You don't know if you've ever seen a look like that coming from another woman. Perhaps it's her staggering beauty or perhaps it's the look of desire and lust on her face. Perhaps it's all of these things and the end of a very long and exhausting night and perhaps it's because you want and need her and feel like you're five minutes away from losing any control you have.

The elevator doors open.

Do you really want to do this?

You don't want to listen to yourself or to anybody else.

It's a hotel in another city and nobody is going to know.

God will know.

But is God going to care? When has he been caring recently and why will he suddenly decide to care now?

You walk down to your hotel room and without a thought slip in the key. The signal sounds its entrance.

"After you," you tell her.

She walks in and you close the door behind you.

All alone.

Just the two of you.

It all comes down to this.

5:48 A.M.

THE HOTEL ROOM FEELS VERY DIFFERENT.

You sit against the edge of the bed. Jasmine walks past, first looking out the window, then glancing around the room.

Your small black suitcase is packed and ready to go. The only thing you will throw in there is your toiletries bag. Your black leather briefcase holds your computer and iPod and Palm Pilot, waiting to be turned on.

Jasmine slips off her light coat, rests it on the chair, then turns around. You see her bare arms, long and perfect, a light and creamy color. Her silk plunging camisole reveals a lot. The jeans she wears look painted on. She glides closer to you and smiles.

She doesn't say a word. But her eyes say it all.

This time it's real.

She is not a nameless face on a magazine or a computer screen. She breathes and talks and looks at you. There is real emotion on her face. Desire, confidence, mischief, even a slight taunt.

She takes your hand.

You know better Michael you know better than this you can't do this there are consequences.

And you think of those faces and bodies you've seen too many times. Nameless. Mindless.

Each one is someone's daughter. Someone's love.

Each one is someone.

You have programmed yourself to think of this as being fantasy, as being make-believe.

"It's okay, Michael," she says, standing over you, holding your hands.

Her voice shows a hint of . . . what? What can it be?

Fear.

But a fear of what? Fear of moving ahead? Fear of being intimate? Fear of

rejection.

You pull back.

"You're shaking," she says.

And you look at your hands. You think of your ring, which is on the desk and not where it should be.

"We shouldn't—"

"Yes, we should," Jasmine says.

"You should probably go."

"Michael, it's fine."

"No, it's not."

"It's *so* fine. Just come here. Don't worry—"

You stand up, then start to back away.

"You have to leave," you tell her.

"We just got here."

"I know, but—"

"It's fine."

"I don't think so."

"Nobody is going to know," she says in what is barely more than a whisper.

Sometime, maybe hours ago, you left reality behind. You left context and motive behind. Tonight you've been running on adrenaline and desire.

It's so strong and so overwhelming and I don't know if I can control it.

Because it's here, right now, right here in front of you.

But you can't. And you won't.

"Jasmine, please."

She slides up to you, against you, and for another moment you wrap your arms around her.

Nobody will ever know.

But that's not the point.

Nobody will ever care.

But you will because you know better.

"It's okay," she says, the voice of someone used to this, the voice of someone who doesn't have any inhibitions.

You breathe in.

"You won't regret it."

But you think of the times you have regretted something. Failing. Looking. Lusting. Wanting something you can't have.

She's not yours.

You know this but still it's so easy so very easy.

She will never be yours.

And you blink and think of Lisa.

The two are not the same. For a man, this is not about affection or love or companionship.

It's about flesh and desire and it's the thing every man has to struggle with.

But here you are in your hotel room smelling her and feeling her touch. How could it have gotten this far?

I was helping her out.

But were you? Wasn't this what you wanted the entire time?

Don't fool yourself, Michael.

And your lips are about to touch hers . . .

No.

And then you pull away.

"Come here," she says.

"No, I can't."

"Michael, you won't—"

"Please, Jasmine. I can't. I'm sorry. I'm married. And I can't—I don't know what I'm doing. What any of this—"

You shake your head, and she comes up to you. "It's okay."

You look away. "No."

She puts a hand against your arm but you jerk it back.

"I'm not going to bite."

She said that hours ago. When you should have known better. When you should have realized where this was going.

You wipe your eyebrows, a nervous affectation that you sometimes can't help. Jasmine is leaning over you, her legs crossed in yours.

"Nobody is ever going to know, Michael," she whispers, her voice warm against your neck. "I know you want this as much as I do."

You breathe in.

God she is beautiful.

Your hands find their way around her again, but you stand up and walk away.

Any second now and it will be too late. Any second and you'll give in.

"Look . . ."

She waits for you now, looking, wondering what you're going to say.

"Please, I'm asking you—I'm sorry. I just—I can't."

She stares at you. There is silence and your eyes find their way back to hers.

And suddenly you see the look on her face.

The desire and the enticement have disappeared. Now all you see is anger.

"Jasmine, I'm—"

"No."

Her voice has changed. Everything about her has changed.

"Look, I'm not rejecting you."

She laughs.

"What?" you ask.

"You could *never* reject me."

"Yeah, okay. And I'm not. It's just—"

"You're pathetic."

You look at her and can't answer her harsh comment.

"I'm sorry," you say again.

She shakes her head, the long blonde hair wrapping itself around one cheek.

I still might change my mind.

"I had high hopes for this night," she says. "You let me down."

She takes her jacket and puts it back on. You go to touch her shoulder, but she shrugs away.

"Look, Jasmine—"

"Please, stop calling me that."

"What do you want me to call you?"

"Nothing," she says, looking at you with cold eyes. "Nothing at all."

You rub your hands against your face and feel like collapsing on the bed. Jasmine starts to go to the door.

"Let me at least walk you out."

She looks at you and laughs. "You so don't get it, do you?"

"Get what?"

"The truth."

You look at her and try to see what she's talking about.

"You're a nice guy. I should've known. I've met a few guys like you. But then again, that was the whole point, wasn't it?"

She opens the door, then looks back at you.

The look on her face isn't kind or cordial. It's more tired and amused.

"Let me—let me walk you out."

"The night is officially over."

"Please . . ."

"You really were a disappointment," she says.

What's that mean?

You get your room key, then follow Jasmine out to the hallway.

You can breathe better out here.

As you wait for the elevator, Jasmine looks at you. Again, something has changed. Something is off.

"Look, I'm sorry," you say.

For what? Saying no? Not giving in? Rejecting her?

"Please," Jasmine says.

"What?"

"You have no idea why I'm even angry."

You nod at her.

She looks as if she has more to say. Then she simply laughs and gets on the elevator by herself.

Her laugh scares you.

6:33 A.M.

YOUR HAND OPENS YOUR HOTEL ROOM DOOR. For a second, you think of Lisa.

You think of the first time with Lisa.

Her lips were soft, her smile genuine, her touch inspiring.

You had never wanted—had never needed someone so bad—as you wanted Lisa. At that moment, at that time.

You had both waited so long and it was the first time.

You could feel your body shake.

And you knew when it was over that it was well worth it. That it was right. That it was fulfilling and that only someone like God could invent this form of love and could give it to you.

The world distorts it and mangles and contorts it. Love and sex and desire and lust and emotion and love.

What is real love?

Saying no.

Saying no more.

Not giving in.

Trying again.

You love Lisa but it's not with the same passion and fire that you had when you first fell in love and when you first married.

Love isn't just about the passion and fire of newlyweds. Some people think it is, and they search and search and try to find it, try to relive it, wanting to capture those brilliant, glorious, ground-swelling moments.

But they can never recapture them.

You know better and know that you've been looking for something to fill you that can't. That absolutely, positively can't.

And you almost gave in, trying to find it. You almost gave yourself over.

6:42 A.M.

Michael Michael Michael

The scent of sweet perfume in the hotel room still lingers. You start to gather your things, knowing you have to leave, knowing you have to get out of here.

She might come back. She might knock on your door again. She might come in. She might do God knows what.

You look at yourself in the mirror. You have to look away.

The suitcase is packed. You gather your bag. You quickly look over the items on the desk.

You don't want the change sitting there. You pick up the extra key card and the key for the minibar.

I've got to get out of here.

You put your briefcase on top of the suitcase and prepare to head out.

Don't go.

You're running late but something is bothering you.

You stop and think.

Then you turn around and look on the desk again.

Underneath the copy of *USA Today* sits something round and golden.

You pick up your wedding ring and slip it back on your finger.

I am such a complete and utter fool.

You look at your hand and see the familiar ring.

Your hand trembles. You try to shake it off, but you can't.

You have everything that you need. You have to get out of here.

7:20 A.M.

THE NECKLACE DANGLES FROM THE MIRROR, and the white cross waves at you. You stare at it, mesmerized, too exhausted to actually feel anything. The outline of the small pendant stands out in front of the cab's windshield, the glow from the sunrise creeping up from the east. The streets are empty this morning, the bridge to the airport and to freedom open to change lanes. The driver still races ahead, oblivious to you and to everything you're leaving behind.

A radio commentator talks but you don't listen.

You see the cross sway back and forth.

As you take the Triborough bridge, you can look to your right and see the shadowed veil of the city, still in lights, still resting, still half awake like it always stays. Ahead, past the cross and the windshield with the cracked hole and the four lanes and the bridge, you see the crest of the sun filling the sky, daring to wake the sleeping apple up.

You feel the wedding ring you almost left behind in the hotel room. Maybe that would have woken *you* up. Seems like nothing else is getting your attention.

What is it about you?

Really. What is it?

Why can't enough simply be *enough*?

Why do you have this restless feeling that doesn't go away?

You know the answers and yet you sometimes ignore them, hoping that work and money and the rest of the world can solve the questions burning deep inside.

Sometimes, when nobody is watching, you try to solve this burning yourself. But losing yourself online in a sea of sin never fulfills you. It only makes you hungrier. And when you quench that thirst momentarily, you try to tell yourself you won't do it again. You try to tell yourself it's okay. You even ask God to forgive you. But will you ever change? Will you ever try to be a better person? Will you ever finally lay it before God and ask him to help you and to change you?

God help me help me God I'm crying out to you I need help.

You don't know what help looks like. You don't know when it will arrive and in what sort of form. You're ashamed and yet too proud to admit this to anybody else. Even Lisa. Even the woman you were supposed to tell everything.

God you know everything.

Every fault and every failure.

Running away doesn't work. Being far from home in a busy, mindless city doesn't work. Being under the shadows in the pit of night doesn't work.

Nothing works.

Surrender all.

You want to keep running. You want to keep hiding. You want to keep playing those games that everybody else plays. Why should you be any different? Any different whatsoever?

Turn your life around and lay it all before his feet. Lay it all before him and find rest and comfort.

The wind blows through the cracked windows as the car races past the side of the bridge, cement and concrete so close to you.

No getting out now.

God you know how foolish I am and nothing or no sin can be hidden from you.

You think of someone else long ago uttering these words.

Don't let the floods overwhelm me or the deep waters swallow me or the pit of death devour me.

All you have to do is call out. Pray and ask for God to help you and find you and forgive you.

Have compassion on me, Lord, for I am weak.

Still weak, still after all this time, after so many years, after pretending to be the adult and the grown-up and the responsible man and a good person.

I am sick at heart. How long, O Lord, until you restore me?

You don't know if you can even ask. This is your fault, your decision that has resulted in this mess. This is something only you can get yourself out of.

You alone know the way I should turn.

You can't turn that way.

Hear my cry, for I am very low.

You breathe in and breathe out and breathe in again and feel the sting of tears in your eyes.

Lord, please forgive me. Please forgive me and let me get out of this mess. Let me make something good out of this, Lord, and help me. Lord, help me.

It's all you can say.

All you can do.

The rest is up to him.

You know he can hear you.

Behind you, behind this taxi, the restless, endless beast of a city begins another day, stretching and waiting to devour another soul.

It tried to devour yours. And it almost succeeded.

But God spared you.

This time.

8:14 A.M.

Sitting down in the airport terminal, resting on a chair across from a businessman reading a paper, sipping on a cup of coffee, you feel the exhaustion stifle you. You feel nauseated, for multiple reasons. You just want to get on the plane and close your eyes and wish for the last twenty-four hours to disappear. From your life and your memory and your very existence.

Life doesn't work like that.

Your phone vibrates in your pocket. For a second you feel a sense of worry.

Reality bites back and it starts now.

It could be any one of a number of people. But you don't recognize the number.

You open up your phone carefully.

"Hello?"

"Michael."

For a moment you think it's Jasmine. But the woman's voice is different. A little lower.

"It's Amanda."

Something happened to Jasmine. Riley ended up hurting her.

"What happened?" she asks.

"What do you mean?"

"I mean—I mean exactly that. What happened?"

"Are you okay?"

The voice on the other end hesitates for a second, as if wondering what you mean.

"Where are you?" she asks.

"The airport."

"You sound bad. Long night?"

She laughs and you find the laughter, the sheer frivolity of her tone, remarkable.

"Why are you calling?" you ask.

"I just spoke to Riley."

Your accomplice. Your partner.

"He says you were waving a gun at him."

Again she laughs.

What does she want?

"So why didn't you go through with it?"

"What are you talking about?" you ask, annoyed but too tired to be angry.

"J's little guinea pig couldn't run up the ladder, could he?"

What is this crazy chick talking about?

"What do you want?"

Amanda pauses for a minute, as though she's driving or doing something.

"I just want to know one thing," Amanda says.

"Where's Jasmine?"

Amanda curses. "Please, stop calling her Jasmine. That's getting old."

"Is she okay?"

"What? Are you still . . . you're actually worried about her?"

Amanda laughs.

"What's so funny?" you ask.

"You."

"Yeah?"

"Yeah. I mean, she did a number on you. I just can't believe you didn't go through with it."

"With what?"

"Tell me one thing. Did you do anything?"

"Do anything?"

"Yeah. You went back to your place, right? So—did you get a souvenir for your troubles? A going-away present?"

"Please."

"Just tell me."

"Nothing happened," you say.

"Seriously?"

"No."

"Wow."

She sounds genuinely surprised.

"What do you want?"

"J won't tell me the truth. She has this tendency to lie.
Especially with bets."

What?

"With what?"

Amanda laughs. "Mister, you need to get on that plane
and never come back to New York."

"What do you mean by 'bets'?"

"I've got to hand it to you, though. Remember what I said
about her getting men to do whatever she asks? She didn't get
it this time."

This time.

The words stun you into silence.

Your hand starts to shake.

This time.

"The girl is creative, but this time it didn't work," Amanda
says.

"This time," you say.

"That's what happens when you have a lot of time on your
hands."

"What?"

Amanda laughs. "You swear you guys didn't—"

"Nothing happened."

"Okay. That's what I needed."

"Wait—hold on."

"What?"

Your mind is reeling with a hundred questions needing answers.

"Was hooking up—was that part of the bet?" you ask.

"That's usually the bet. But this time, we made it a little more . . . interesting."

"Interesting how?"

"Doesn't matter," Amanda says. "J lost."

"Those guys at the club. At Exit. Who were they?"

"Bad habits and parents who don't pay bills."

"What?"

"Use your imagination. It's not that hard. Look, I gotta—"

"Who were the guys who held me up at gunpoint? Dropped me off in the middle of nowhere?"

"J's bodyguards. They hate it when she disappears."

"What'd they have against me?" you ask.

"They were probably trying to scare you. They were just playing. But the guys at the club—J didn't see that coming tonight. But it made things more—well, I'll say it again. More interesting."

"Was Jasmine ever in danger?"

Amanda sounds like she's outside walking now. "Depends on who you ask."

"Meaning?"

"Her parents think she needs to be in rehab. But besides that, no, not really. Those guys won't hurt her. Now guys like you, they will."

"And Riley?"

"He's probably the only decent thing that's happened to her in a long time. God knows he's tried and tried again with her. But that's why J's so sick and twisted."

"Why's that?" you ask.

"Because she tried to get you to kill him. And all for what? Just a bet. Which . . . I . . . won."

Amanda curses and laughs. Before you can say anything, the line goes dead.

You sit and stare at the phone.

You have nothing left. No energy, no emotion, no expression, nothing left.

But the fear still resides deep down.

And it's starting to bubble again.

People pass, and you wish you could be like one of them, nameless and faceless and blameless.

All of us are blameless.

But not today. Not today.

Today you are to blame.

8:49 A.M.

THE FIRST THING YOU NOTICE as you pass her by are sky-blue eyes that linger for a while as she greets you. Long, straight molasses hair is gathered in a clip and falls neatly behind her dark blue suit. You fall into a seat and sigh. You still can't believe you're here, on this plane, ready to take off.

For a few moments you sit there, wondering if anybody is going to sit next to you. Thankfully, nobody does.

What are you going to tell Lisa? You don't know. You really don't know.

Something almost happened but does that make it any better that it didn't happen? I still tried and still went looking for something to possibly happen.

You close your eyes but continue to see Jasmine's face, her

cold look as she got into the elevator. You hear Amanda's laugh and her casual confession.

I don't get it. I really don't get it.

The plane soon takes off and you feel glad when it is up in the air and the wheels are pulled in and you're heading home.

You look up the aisle with two seats on each side and see a young woman glance at you and smile. It's an innocent smile, the kind that might say *You look tired* or *I'd like to get to know you* or a hundred other statements. A sweet, innocent smile.

Perhaps there is nothing innocent about another woman's smile.

You close your eyes and see Lisa in your mind. Her sweet smile, every intention known, every desire well placed.

You wonder if you should say anything.

You know you're not a bad man, an evil man, a typical man. But you're still a sinner. Still flawed. Still blinded by desires that sometimes brush by like the touch of a stranger on a city street.

Sleep should come but doesn't. In the darkness you see Jasmine's eyes, her smile, her glance beckoning you to come.

You hear her laugh.

They all mock you.

You know they will haunt you for some time.

Why? Why did this all happen?

You don't know why. You don't know much of anything anymore.

But you know that the two things you need the most in your life now—God and Lisa—are the two things you've overlooked for a long time.

I'm sorry.

I'm so sorry.

You look out the window to the skies and the heavens and know that he's hearing you. And that forgiveness is something that is not optional. Forgiveness is essential.

You know you need to speak the same words to Lisa. And to try, after all this time, to start again.

Your eyes grow heavy, and for the first time in twenty-four hours you drift off to sleep.

SOMETIME BETWEEN
9:37 - 9:45 A.M.

"TALK TO ME."

Her voice is a whisper, a soft petal floating down in your dream as you hover somewhere high in the clouds.

Is she really right there next to you?

Is she really at your side, not abandoning you?

"I'm here."

It's dark, but you can make out the line of Lisa's face against her pillow and under the covers.

"You're still here," you say.

"I'm always going to be here."

"I'm sorry," you say.

"It's okay."

"No, it's not."

"I love you."

"I'm sorry, Lisa. I'm just—I'm going to change."

"I know you want to."

"I just—sometimes I feel locked up. Sometimes I feel so—I don't know. I struggle so much."

"But you're trying to make this work."

"Feels like I haven't for some time."

"We'll get through this," Lisa says.

You feel her hand touch yours and clench it.

"I thought—I hoped—things would be different if we had kids."

"They are."

"But—I know—but—I just, I'm praying that God will . . . I don't know . . . really get through to me."

"He will."

But how, you wonder in the silence of your bedroom.

How will God get through to you when you don't want to listen to him? When you are running away from him? When nothing gets your attention anymore? When you're jaded and busy and when life is overwhelming?

So in the silence of your room, with Lisa still at your side, still your wife and your partner, you pray. It's the first time you've prayed in a long time.

Lord, do something in me to get my attention, to bring me back closer to you. Help me to be a better person, to be a better husband, a better man.

You still feel Lisa's touch. You don't deserve it. You don't deserve her.

Help me to love her more and help me to love myself and this world less.

It's a simple prayer.

Lord do something in my life to change me.

9:46 A.M.

A SLIGHT DROP WAKES YOU UP.

You remember that moment between Lisa and yourself.

You remember that prayer.

You realize that God answered it in the strangest of ways.

10:20 A.M.

THE CITYSCAPE OF CHICAGO is in full view from your tiny window. The plane circles the city and you look down to see the great waters of Lake Michigan. Sun is piercing the buildings and they glow in the midmorning light.

You think of going back home. Of greeting Lisa and embracing the kids.

What is there to tell? To say?

I want a change, Lord.

And you don't know exactly what that means. Maybe it's in some of the late-night habits you have. Maybe it's in the way you view the rest of the world.

Maybe it's with Lisa.

But what do you want?

Maybe it's not necessarily about me.

You have lived with this woman for some time and have loved and supported and provided for her. But . . .

I want to be her friend again.

The high-rise buildings and skyscrapers pass by and you feel their comforting familiarity.

The suburbs, sprawled out for miles, the endless towns with so many lives, so many people, so many individuals.

This is the life you've made and the life you've been given, Michael. Be happy with it. Be thankful for it.

You might not be sitting here on this plane. One slight step or detour and everything could be over.

You breathe in. You look at your hands and can feel them trembling.

So many things await you down there.

A job that needs figuring out. A company that thought it knew where it was going and now has to start over. You'll develop a new plan and try for the best. But you'll be starting at square one.

Square one.

Then there's the family that needs figuring out. And more specifically, a marriage that has needed CPR for some time.

Good friends from church can't help. Counseling can't help. Even every little thing you've tried to do can't help. You can't solve this.

You don't want to admit it but there is really only one way.

God I need you now and I need you more than ever before.

A packed interstate passes by below. Thousands of people like you, trying to live their lives the best way they can, are waiting, hoping for the best but making dumb decisions and living with those consequences.

Help me to know what to do and where to go.

Because you know Lisa is ultimately not the answer.

Your kids—as much as you love them and as much as they are a part of your very being and the very fabric of your soul—are not the answer.

A bank account and a secure job and a home are definitely not the answers.

And wandering around, flailing around in the darkness, trying to desperately look for something that fulfills you . . . none of these things are the answer.

I am.

As passengers begin filing off the plane, you stand and begin walking and see the cute attendant looking at you with a grin.

"Is this home for you?" she casually asks.

"Yes, it is," you say.

"Then welcome home."

"Thanks."

You walk through the gate and through the masses at O'Hare and go toward baggage claim. You turn on your phone, and a few minutes later you feel the vibrating call coming in.

You look at the phone and feel your heart tighten.

There is one name on the phone.

Lisa.

You look at the phone, eager to hear her voice, eager to talk to her, eager to try and figure out a way to make things work for the two of you.

Today is the first day of the rest of your life.

It's a saying you've heard before. And today, that saying fits.

"Hey, stranger," the voice says.

Hearing it is soothing. You just want to take her in your arms and never let go.

"Hi."

"You sound tired."

"Long night."

"The kids miss you."

"I miss them." You pause for a moment, then add, "I miss you."

Lisa laughs. "You weren't gone long enough to miss me."

I've been gone for some time.

She talks about going to the grocery store and the day ahead and how the kids are doing. You listen attentively as you walk toward the baggage claim.

"So I'll see you soon, right?"

"Very soon," you say. "It'll be nice to be back home."

"I'll say. Having you around will give me a little break."

"I love you, Lisa," you say.

"You too," she says automatically.

But you know you love Lisa. Sometimes a saying and a feeling and a life can be taken for granted. Sometimes it takes almost losing it all to know what you have and appreciate all you've been given.

You walk to get to your luggage and wait for a moment.

You have your iPod on and scroll through the songs. You find a familiar song that you haven't heard for some time. It seems appropriate enough.

The guitar starts sweet enough, until the heavier guitar and drums come pounding in. Then you hear Billy Corgan singing. *Today is the greatest day I've ever known.*

A new day. Another day to try again, to make amends, to keep going.

Today.

And today you're asking—you're praying—for a change.

ACKNOWLEDGMENTS

To all of you:

Mom, Dad, Sharon, Andy McGuire, LB Norton, Claudia Cross, Keri Tryba, Barry Smith, my small group, my colleagues, and my fans.

Thanks.

TRAVIS THRASHER has worked in the publishing industry for over a dozen years and is the author of seven novels. He travels extensively and has fortunately never had a layover in New York City. He and his wife live in the Chicago suburbs. For more information on Travis, go to www.TravisThrasher.com or email him at TT@Tyndale.com.

More from Travis Thrasher . . .

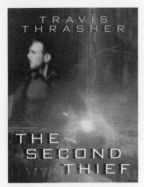

ISBN: 0-8024-1707-8

The Second Thief

Meet Tom Ledger. Disillusioned. Bored. Willing to sell his soul—or at least his company's most guarded secrets—to the highest bidder. Tom has no way of knowing that within hours of committing his first felony he'll be catapulted into a high-stakes drama as the airplane he's on drops like a rock into a Nebraska cornfield.

Gun Lake

Five escaped convicts looking for freedom. A woman on the run from another life. A father carrying sins of the past. A broken county deputy who can become a hero. And a dangerous ringleader who will bring all their paths together.

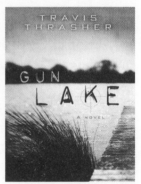

ISBN: 0-8024-1748-5

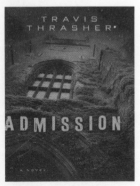

ISBN: 0-8024-8671-1

Admission

Jake Rivers has it all. One last semester of college. A close-knit group of friends. The love of his life he's nearly won over. A promising future almost here. Until something unspeakable happens and his life, and the lives of his friends, are changed forever.

COMING SOON FROM TRAVIS THRASHER . . .

ISOLATION

THE MILLERS ARE A MISSIONARY FAMILY on a much-needed fur-
lough from Papua New Guinea. James is trying not to lose his
faith. Stephanie is struggling not to lose her mind.

Stephanie feels like she's seeing things. Strange and scary
things. Blood dripping down the walls of their house. One of
her children suffocating. Are these nightmares or premoni-
tions? Looking for a chance to regroup and reload, they move
into a lodge in the hills of North Carolina designed for families like theirs.

And then the storm comes. They are isolated with no one
else anywhere near them. Or so they think.

Isolation will be available in stores everywhere January, 2007.

PROLOGUE
(FIFTEEN YEARS AGO)

IT WAS THE SORT OF HOT SUMMER NIGHT that made a young woman abandon her fears and jump into the lake with barely anything on. And the sort of night that made a man in the nearby woods watch.

He heard their voices first. Laughter, conversation, even shouts, as if there wasn't another soul in the surrounding countryside. The night air was thick and the forest full of aged trees and wild growth. It was easy to be swallowed in the black pit of the woods. And easy to observe.

He watched as one thing led to another, and a bet turned into a splash, and then the girl shouted as the boy ran off, leaving the swimmer all alone.

She didn't seem to mind. The moon lit the murky waters of the lake, the ripples gliding out from the arms and feet that calmly stretched out. She looked peaceful. Peaceful and very naive.

He watched from behind a nearby oak tree, wondering when the girl would come out, knowing that would be the time to make his move. He was used to walking in shadows, walking without sound, walking without anyone knowing.

For several moments he held his breath.

He waited, his eyes unmoving, his hands flexing.

He had killed before. And tonight he would kill again.

Nobody knew. Nobody understood the hunger, the need, the curiosity, what it felt like to hear the screams, the sensation of control.

It was all about control and he was in control and tonight he would control again.

The sound of the water spattering fell over the backdrop of the Michigan night. Summer nights were supposed to feel carefree just like the picture. Nobody expected people like him to be out there, to be around, to be watching.

But there were plenty of people like him. People with hunger. People with need.

He watched carefully.

Waiting.

"Hey."

The voice came out of nowhere. It didn't jolt him, but merely annoyed him. He turned around from the tree he stood next to and looked into the darkness behind him.

He couldn't see anybody.

"Yeah, you. I'm looking at you."

The voice sounded young but undaunted, defiant.

"Having a nice little time hiding out here?"

He could see the figure come in better view. The light of the moon reflected on the forehead, the intense eyes, the strong cheek bones.

"What do you think you're doing?" the voice asked.

"You'd be wise to sneak back into those woods and never come out again," he told the intruder.

He could feel his hands flex, getting eager, getting ready.

The tall figure continued to approach.

"I know about you," the voice said, suddenly sounding different, sounding lower.

Lower. Or, fuller.

"I know all about you."

And then the figure was up to him, swiftly just like that, a shadow blurring and suddenly in his own, up against him, over him.

He didn't feel the knife until it was plunged deep into his gut. Again. And again.

"I know all about you," the deep, full, guttural voice said. "And you're no longer needed."

He dropped on his back and looked up at the face of a man that looked like a boy and he could see the smile and then he looked further up into the heavens and even though the stars were out all he could see was a growing flood of darkness and for a brief second he felt a dread come into him worse than any feeling in his life. He knew that he was done but that the terror had just started.

PART ONE: DIVISION
CHAPTER 1: THE STRANGER IN THE HOUSE

THE LOUD CRASH WOKE STEPHANIE. It came from outside their bedroom, but she wasn't sure where. She jerked and turned over on her back, her eyes opened and adjusting to the pitch black. Next to her, Jim's heavy sleep floated somewhere between snoring and ragged breathing. She called out his name twice but he wouldn't wake at this hour of the night unless she tugged at him for a few minutes. He was a big man who didn't go to sleep easily, but once he did he stayed asleep.

I know I heard something and it sounded like it came from down the hall.

She slipped out of the massive covers of the bed and felt

the chill of the winter night greet her. Stephanie thought of Zachary and Ashley, still adjusting to being in separate rooms after being cramped together in their tiny room in Dambi. One day they might know what it felt like to have their own home. Not someone else's house they were staying in or a house they were renting or a house they had built on the field that would be temporary. She wanted stability, something she could see every day for ten years, maybe something she could grow old in.

The wind blew hard against the house and she wondered if it was still snowing. The first few days in January had been particularly brutal, and they were forecasting another round of snow for Chicago this weekend.

I know I heard something and I know I'm awake this time I'm not sleep walking.

The handle felt hard and cold as she turned it and opened the door. The slight creak wouldn't change Jim's snores. She walked down the hallway, a small night light illuminating the floor as she got to Ashley's room. This house had four bedrooms, amazingly, so they had put Ash in the room closest to them. Sometimes she still wanted to sleep with them, a habit that was hard to break and even harder to argue with now that they were in a new house. They had been here since September, but it still didn't feel like home. The furniture had been picked out by someone years ago and showed it. The house itself felt like a model home, one of those you toured through and looked at but never *lived* in. It looked like it was trying to have the feel of a home but didn't get it. And as much as the Millers had tried to make this their home, it still never felt like that for Stephanie.

Ashley was in her bed with half the covers off. Stephanie put them back over her and made sure she could hear her breathing. She always did that with her kids, even though they were five and eight. Ashley was the baby and always would be.

What about another one?

She could hear Jim's voice and question but knew she was through. She didn't want another child even though she dearly loved both of them. Men just didn't understand and could never understand the pain and the emotional journey of having a baby. Stephanie sometimes wondered if she was selfish, but then knew that she couldn't go through another nine months of that if she had doubts.

She walked down to Zachary's room and walked inside. It felt colder for some reason, and she couldn't help but shiver as she entered the room.

Zach breathed heavily, but that was only because he was coming off a nasty sinus infection. Everything in the room looked fine. There was a small night-light in each of the kids' rooms, so she could see Zachary under the covers with his eyes closed and his dark brown hair messy.

Her heart moved a little looking at him and she knew as always that even though she wasn't supposed to have a favorite, she loved Zachary a little more than Ashley. She would never tell another soul this but she knew that God could see this and she often wondered if it was wrong having a favorite. She couldn't help it. Zachary was her first and had been an answer to prayer and was also just . . . he was Zach.

He was special. For some reason, reasons she couldn't always articulate even to herself, Zachary was not like any other kid Stephanie had been around. Ashley took after her father, but Zach didn't necessarily take after either of them.

He's so much like you it's scary.

She could hear Jim telling her this but sometimes she didn't know. Zach was restless and outgoing and inquisitive and feisty and all those things. So, yes, sure, he took more after her than Jim's quiet and deep persona. But there was something about Zach that wasn't anything like her, that wasn't like anybody.

He's a fifty-year-old man in the body of an eight-year-old.

She was lost looking at her son when she heard another noise. This one came from downstairs, in the kitchen, and it sounded like something fell over.

That's twice now and I know someone's here—someone's in our house.

Her heart raced and she tiptoed to the top of the stairs where she just stood and listened. She wondered about racing down to get Jim, but then she knew he would think she was sleepwalking and would tell her just to go back to bed. Sure, she had dreams—nightmares—every now and then but this was real. She was awake. Her bare feet could feel the soft carpet underneath them, something that was foreign and took awhile to get used to since coming off the missionary field. Her eyes had adjusted to the darkness. She looked downstairs but could see nothing.

She slowly made her way down the steps, one after another. *Someone's down there,* she knew, she believed.

So why was she walking down there? She was the mother of the house. This was crazy. *If* someone was down there, she shouldn't be going down there to see them, to greet them.

But she made it to the bottom of the stairs. She held her breath and listened. Nothing. Her hands shook and she couldn't see anything except the light on the VCR saying the time of 3:14 a.m.

She turned on the light and expected to see a man in black standing in the middle of the kitchen. Her heart raced and she stood there at the base of the stairs, the light illuminating both the family room and the kitchen.

Nobody.

Stephanie walked over to the kitchen and stood in the middle near the island, looking around to see if anybody was there. Or if anything had fallen. There was nobody to see and nothing on the wood floor. No stray pot that had fallen or pan that was out of place.

She needed to calm down. She opened the refrigerator door to get some milk but then saw something out of the corner of her eye.

Something shadowy and black and big and quick.

Something going up the stairs.

She stood there for a moment, not sure what she had just seen.

It was a blur, but it had been something.

She heard movement on the carpeted steps, as though it was Jim heading up the stairs.

The footsteps were quick, like someone was running.

Stephanie's body froze and she could only turn her head.

She saw the set of knives that she used often in cooking, one of the few things she enjoyed doing in this house. For one brief second, she couldn't move or think or do anything. But then she heard the steps find their way to the hallway

to the kids' rooms

and with the sound of the creak in the hallway right outside of Zach's room, Stephanie jolted herself into motion and moved without thinking.

She grabbed the largest knife in the set and gripped it as she ran up the stairs.

It took her less than a second to get to the top.

She rushed into Zach's room and held the knife out in the darkness. She turned around, expecting to see somebody. Nobody was there.

She ran down to Ashley's room but it was the same.

Nobody.

I know what I heard and what I saw. I know it.

She stood in the middle of Ashley's room, looking toward the doorway and to the hallway outside.

Suddenly, she saw a figure glide by.

She felt very cold, a cold deep under her skin.

Stephanie charged out of the room and rushed down the hallway to Zach's room. She looked in his room and found the bed missing, the covers turned over, the room empty.

She felt the bed but nothing was there.

For a second she just stood there in horror.

He's gone somebody took him the darkness took him he's gone he's forever gone

And she couldn't help but feel her legs get weak until she

had to kneel on the ground. She took in a breath and felt light-headed but she kept the knife in her hand.

Where'd he go where'd they take him?

And as she panted for air a sound came from behind her and she jerked around with her knife facing the doorway and suddenly she found herself blinded by bright lights and she squinted and made out an ominous figure at the doorway.

"Don't! I swear!" she said, squinting her eyes and waving the knife toward the doorway.

"Steph—what the—Stephanie, drop the knife!"

She looked up and saw the beard first and then saw the eyes, bigger than usual. The voice hadn't just asked her to drop the knife. It had been a command, a deep and booming command that jerked her

awake?

and made her drop the knife.

Jim stood at the doorway and the light to Zach's room was on.

Jim came to her side and picked up the knife.

"What are you doing?" he asked her as he helped her up.

"It's Zach—I saw someone—heard something—then I looked and someone was coming up—I didn't know—"

She looked behind and saw Zach in his bed, his hair shaped in a mushroom, his eyes wide and open and adjusting to the light.

He's there.

"He wasn't—I looked and he wasn't there. Jim, I swear, I saw something. I know I did. I don't know what—"

"What are you doing with the knife?"

"I was scared somebody—"

"Steph. You gotta get some help. This is really . . . "

He stopped himself because Zachary was hanging on every word. Jim put the knife on top of the small dresser and then went over to Zach. He sat next to him.

"Hey, buddy. It's okay. Mommy was just having another dream."

But I wasn't dreaming this time I swear I wasn't dreaming.

"It's okay. Just go to sleep. All right?"

Zach just nodded and then he looked at her.

"Mom, are you okay?"

She stood up and she could feel her legs shaking. "I'm fine. I'm sorry, sweetheart. I'm just tired."

As she went to kiss Zach, she could see his frightened look.

He's frightened of me. Oh dear God he's frightened of me.

"Get some sleep buddy. Okay?"

Jim tucked him in and then took the knife off the dresser. He turned off the lights and went downstairs to put the knife away.

Stephanie found her way back to bed. She lay on her back, feeling as awake as she had been when she first heard the noise or saw the figure.

Jim came back in the room and didn't bother turning on the light. He climbed back in bed and for a minute was quiet.

"Jim?"

"Yeah," he eventually said.

"I'm sorry."

There was more silence, and she wondered what he was thinking.

"Jim?"

"Let's just get some rest, okay?"

"I heard something. I know you think I was sleepwalking, but I heard something."

She could tell Jim was thinking, wondering whether to say something. He was a man who rarely said something he didn't want to say.

"James?" she asked, changing the name to try and get him to respond.

"I just found you in our son's room, hovering over him with a knife. *With a knife.*"

A fear raced through Stephanie, and it wasn't at Jim's words. It was at the way he said them. He spoke them as though he was angry at her, as though she was a stranger and not the woman he loved and who had given birth to these children.

The thing that scared her the most was that she could hear the fear in Jim's voice.

Jim was never scared. Of anything.

And now . . .

Jim sounded scared.

Of her.